SHERWOOD

SIERRA SIMONE

PROLOGUE

FIVE YEARS earlier

"Don't go," I said to the soldier in front of me.

She stepped inside the house, leaving her bag of olive drab canvas propped against the doorframe.

"I came to say goodbye to your parents," she said.

But it must have been a lie; the way her eyes burned along my body, from my ballet flats to the ribbon holding back my hair, told me it was a lie. Robin Loxley's mother was close with mine, yes, but I knew that Robin had already said goodbye to her yesterday. I knew that she must have already marked how quiet the house was right now. How empty.

"They're not here," I said, instinctively taking a step backward. Not to create space between us, but to invite her inside.

Robin—Lox to everyone who wasn't her grandparents —stepped forward. Brown combat boots, camo-covered body. Her red hair was pulled into a neat ponytail at the nape of her neck, and the collar of her uniform emphasized the line of her jaw and the length of her neck. Her lips were their natural pale mauve today, not painted in the shades of crimson and currant she typically favored.

Her eyelashes were as red as her hair.

"I suppose I'll just have to say goodbye to you alone, then," she murmured, taking another step closer. "I'm not interrupting anything, am I?"

"No," I whispered. "Just packing for college." She was close enough now that I could smell her—cedar and fog and moss—and I wondered if she knew, if she could possibly know how much I loved her. Had always loved her. From our childhood summers in the forest until the day she left for MIT, she had been the rolling, rushing, frothing hope of my heart, a tide that had started as a little girl smitten with her playmate and had churned itself into a powerful, hungry current.

And now here she was, about to leave, about to be deployed, her green eyes like the forest itself come to life, and she was so close now, closer to me than she'd been in years.

"You're flushing," she murmured. "Are you feeling well?"

"I am."

She pressed a hand to my cheek. The shock of her skin on mine was enough to make me inhale. "It's a very pretty flush, Marian."

What else could I whisper but, "Thank you"?

"I like the way you thank me," she replied. Her hand slid to my jaw, and then to my neck. I could feel her fingers toying with the ribbon which held my hair in a loose ponytail. It felt almost like she was holding *me by* my hair, like she could pull on it at any moment to make me do what she wanted—and it felt so powerfully, wonderfully right.

Heat burned up my thighs and tugged low in my stomach. I knew, without even checking, that if she looked down, she'd be able to see my nipples beading through my dress.

Kiss me, I wanted to plead. *Kiss me hard. Kiss me like you're going to war.*

She was close enough now that I could observe the precise slopes of her mouth, the peaks of her Cupid's bow, the concavity of her philtrum. Sunlight caught on her eyelashes, glimmers of gold among the red.

It couldn't be, could it? After years of loving her, wanting her, years of wondering if she even remembered me? Could she really be this close? Touching me?

Staring at me with dark eyes and parted lips?

Kiss me, and don't ask when you do it. Kiss me and take me, kiss me and make me.

I didn't understand what it was that I wanted exactly, why my entire body keened for something more than the sweetness you were supposed to want from a crush, but perhaps it was that I knew that any sweetness wouldn't really be *her*, it would only be a facade. A filtered act. And the thought of anything between us, facades or filters, was anathema to me.

Or maybe I knew even then that sweetness wasn't enough for *me*. How could it be, when it felt so half done, so anemic and feeble? I wanted to wear the memories of a kiss on my skin, I wanted someone's hunger to break on me like a wave on the shore.

But I didn't know how to say any of that back then, and I didn't even know what to hint at—what to intimate and suggest with my expression or with my body language.

All I could do was reach for Lox's hand and wrap it around my ponytail myself.

Her hand tightened without me having to do anything more, and she searched my face, which was now held captive for her examination.

"Think carefully about this," she said slowly.

My reply was immediate. "I don't need to."

And then without any further warning, her mouth pressed down on mine, unlike any kiss I'd ever had before. Her tongue demanded entry, searching out every corner of my mouth once she pushed her way inside, and never had I realized that someone could part my mouth, that someone could spread it, play with it, make use of it.

My mouth could be used.

The revelation of it was shocking, almost breathtaking in its implications. I knew what oral sex was, of course, but my experience had been limited to hearsay and fanfiction, and in those two things, there'd always been a veneer of generosity over the act. You *gave* oral, like a gift, and it was gratefully received: a kindness, a benefaction.

But.

But I could be *used* for oral. Someone could hold me by the hair, just like Lox was doing now, and then they could fuck my mouth. I could be an accessory, a plaything—and I trembled just thinking about it.

She cupped my breast, hard enough to make me gasp, and she smiled against my mouth at the sound. "Too hard, little fox?"

"Never," I panted. She bit my lower lip in response. "Never."

She pulled back to look at me, those eyes again flicking over my face like she was trying to gauge if I were telling the truth or not. A sharp, icy fear splintered through my chest at the idea that she might stop, and before she could, before she could step away, say goodbye, *leave*, I did the only thing I could think of. The only thing that made sense, and then the only thing I wanted to do for the rest of my life.

I sank to my knees in front of her.

"Marian," she said.

Nothing else.

Her hand was still in my hair.

"Let me," I whispered. "Let me."

She didn't speak...but she moved a single booted foot to the side and widened her stance. And when I reached for the buttons of her ACU jacket, she didn't stop my hands. She didn't stop me from unbuttoning the jacket and parting the fabric to reveal a neatly tucked T-shirt, and she didn't stop me from working open the ribbed nylon belt threaded through the loops of her trousers.

With her hand still in my hair, I exposed her, getting her pants open and far enough down her thighs that I could see red curls and the barest hint of slick, pink skin. She slid her fingers in my mouth, pressing down on my tongue, as if seeing how wide I could open, and then she said, "Suck."

And I did, I sucked on her fingers until her eyes were darker than I'd ever, ever seen them.

She abruptly pulled her fingers free and pushed my face against her cunt. Her ACU pants kept her from opening her thighs as wide as would be convenient, but she didn't seem to care if it was convenient for me or not. She held me there until I found an angle that worked, until I pressed hard enough to find what she wanted me to find.

When I eagerly licked at the hard pearl of her clit, she grunted my name. Breathless and wounded, like I'd just kicked her in the stomach.

I was kneeling on the floor, my dress spilling around my knees and my hair mussed and my lipstick all over my face, her camo everywhere and her belt hanging open, and I didn't think heaven could be any better than this. Any better than Lox's hot cunt, the way she fucked my mouth as if she'd paid for it—and the noises she made as I let her, harsh and soft, harsh and soft.

I had no idea what I was doing, had never gone down on anyone before, but that didn't matter, not like this. I wasn't fucking Lox—*she* was fucking *me*; I wasn't giving her a gift, because she was taking it. She rode my tongue, she held me close when she wanted me to suck, pulled my hair when she wanted more of it, or harder.

"Lick," she'd tell me, and I would. "Suck," she'd order next, and I'd do it, happily, happily. And even though I wanted to press my hands against her firm thighs and feel the fabric of her combat uniform against my palms—even though I wanted to run my fingertips over her curls, wanted to slide my touch into the wet clutch of her—I somehow knew that wasn't permitted. That if she wanted it, she'd ask for it, but otherwise I was to remain a willing and pretty mouth for her pleasure.

I could have stayed that way for hours. For days and weeks and the rest of my life.

But finally—with her hand on the back of my head still holding me tight to her—she shuddered once, twice, and came. She continued to fuck me as she did, as if to wring every last ounce of her climax from my willing mouth, and then she let out a long and shaky sigh.

Her hand loosened in my hair. And then she let go.

I looked up at her, my mouth wet, my chin wet too, and I knew my lipstick was everywhere, I knew that my hair was no longer in its ponytail and was tangled in knots where it hung down my back. I knew that she could see down the bodice of my dress, where my nipples had pulled taut enough to hurt, and I knew she could see the way my thighs rubbed together in a mindless search for friction.

And the same way I knew I hadn't been allowed to touch her, I knew I should not touch myself, at least not until she permitted me to. But I wanted to, I wanted to so badly, and it would take nothing, just the graze of my fingers against my own sex, and I'd come right here at her feet.

Her belt and pants still hung open, her pussy still exposed, and the world itself felt newly washed and ripe with possibility, like I could reach out and pluck my own future from the air itself, and that future would be this, more of this. Being hers, being hers in a way that would mean kneeling whenever she wanted me to, and it didn't matter that she was leaving for some far-flung base or that I was going to college, she would come back for me. She would write and call, and somehow we'd make more moments like this, moments even rougher and even more wonderful.

I smiled, and she sucked in a breath.

And then the world darkened once more.

"I'm sorry," she said, zipping up her pants and tucking in her shirt. "I'm sorry, Marian."

"Don't—"

She was pulling her belt tight now and buttoning up her jacket. The front door still hung open behind her, and I had the abrupt awareness that anyone could have seen what we'd just done. My parents were gone for the day, and the front door was sheltered from the road, but it was still a dizzying realization, and I didn't know whether it was disorienting or *terrifying* that we'd been so caught up in the moment that she'd fucked me in front of an open door.

I was still on my knees when she finished dressing. Something unreadable passed over her face as she looked at me, and then she turned away.

"Lox," I begged, but I still didn't get off my knees.

Not that it mattered.

She left anyway.

FIVE YEARS later

Lox came back to Sherwood on a Thursday—the same Thursday that I knelt on a polished concrete floor and kissed the hand-stitched toe box of Rafe de Lacy's shoe.

I suppose it wouldn't have made a difference if I'd known she was back. It had been five years, after all, and she'd been the one to leave Sherwood in the first place. And I was many, many things—young, submissive, obsessive—but the one thing I'd never been, not even as a smitten teenage girl, was foolish. And I had no interest in chasing heartbreak with humiliation.

No thief was good enough to steal the same heart twice.

Or at least so I thought.

CHAPTER

ONE

PRESENT DAY

I knew from the moment he walked in that he was a wolf.

The red-hued lights of the club cast his face mostly in shadow, but I saw enough to sketch a suggestion of his features: a bladed nose, a firm mouth with a certain sharpness to its shape. Heavy-lidded eyes which seemed to take in everything at once, and dark stubble covering the pale cut of his jaw and hollows of his cheeks.

He had the suit, shoes, and watch of a wealthy man; he had the stride and bearing of a powerful one. But it was the sleepless smudges under his eyes that snared me for real, because with them, he looked halfway to unraveling. He looked haunted and wild.

He looked like a lean winter wolf, ready to devour anything just to ease the hunger inside.

Rafe de Lucy, the bartender told me. A guest member at

The Knot, here the last four nights. Visiting from Seattle for some EPA survey thing.

I supposed that I wasn't surprised to have someone new here in Sherwood. Even though it was in the middle of Olympic nowhere, it was the only decent-sized town along this side of the national forest, and where most people ended up staying if they had business or pleasure in these parts. But I was surprised that he was *here*, spending his evenings at The Knot when surely Seattle had a more varied buffet for the seasoned kinkster. When surely it would be easier to wait until he was back home and on his own territory to slake his kinky thirst.

I wondered if he'd be in Sherwood for long...although I wasn't sure if that information mattered or not. I'd only just scraped together the courage to come to the club tonight—and even *that* had taken five years—and as soon as I'd arrived, I'd known I'd made a mistake in coming.

I wasn't ready yet. Maybe I'd never be ready.

Maybe Lox had broken something inside me that would never be fixed.

But when the wolf turned and fixed me with eyes such a blue that they hardly seemed real, being broken stopped mattering. Abruptly, nothing mattered at all—not my company's eternal uphill climb, not the grief from my parents' deaths, not the jagged hole Lox had made when she left Sherwood and took my naive, teenage heart with her.

The only things that mattered were those eyes, those lips. That hunger.

Music slid through the room as the wolf and I stared at each other; distantly, I heard the cries of someone getting spanked in a corner somewhere. Rafe de Lacy tilted his head the smallest amount, looking more like a wolf than ever as he took in the noise around him, but his gaze stayed on me. His hooded eyes narrowed for a moment before he seemed to come to some kind of decision. He turned and walked away, breaking our connection and sending icy disappointment crashing through me.

I took in a steadying breath, reminding myself that I didn't care about some strange dominant I'd never met before. I didn't care if he was interested in me or not. I hadn't wanted to come tonight anyway, and I definitely wasn't ready to try this kink thing for real, not without Lox. And I—

The wolf paused his stride and looked back over his shoulder at me. He canted his head toward a private room in an unmistakable invitation.

You coming or not? the gesture asked.

He didn't bother to wait for my response.

I was off the barstool and following him before I even registered that I'd made my choice. My heels clicked on the wide, wooden floorboards as I walked across the yawning central hall of the club, and curious eyes burned along my skin as I walked through the clumps of people talking, kissing, playing.

Me at The Knot...of course they would stare.

I was still Marian Fitzwalter, after all.

THE PRIVATE ROOM was deceptively spacious and outfitted with a dizzying array of whips, canes, floggers, and several other things I didn't know the names for. There was a bed made up with sheets of dark green silk, a leather spanking bench, and a suspended fireplace in the corner, its flames casting dangerous shadows everywhere. Like the rest of the club, there were exposed wooden beams and large windows looking out over the ocean—the same sort of Pacific-lodge-meets-modernism aesthetic that dominated most of the architecture here in Sherwood.

Rafe de Lacy had ignored everything else in the room and had sat in a black damask chair near the fireplace, his feet planted on the polished concrete floor and his elbows braced on his suit-clad thighs as he leaned forward to look at me. His posture was alert and focused, but there was a restlessness to it too, as if it took everything he had to stay still. Those light blue eyes glittered at me as I shut the door and turned to face him.

"I—" I stopped, my voice sounding ridiculous in the near-silence of the space. I dug my teeth into my lower lip and searched for the right words to say, the right things to do.

But the truth was that I'd never done this before, and not only *this*, with a stranger in a strange place, but real kink at all. What had happened between me and Lox all those years ago had been the furthest thing from planned or rehearsed, and there'd been no protocols or etiquette. Only wordless, shapeless instinct.

It hadn't even been until my sophomore year in college that I'd learned there was a name for it at all.

Rafe de Lacy didn't move or speak in response to my aborted greeting, but neither did he lift his eyes from me. I was pinned in place by that stare, stuck like gravity itself had reoriented at his will, and it reminded me so forcefully —so viscerally—of Lox, that my voice came back, as if summoned by an order.

"I'm not sure what to do next," I admitted. "If I should stand or sit or kneel."

Between his thighs, there was the tiniest flex of his

fingers. "Have you ever knelt for someone before?" His voice was deep, rasping. Faintly British.

"Yes," I answered honestly. "Once."

"Only once?"

"It was a long time ago. It—" I glanced down at the floor, not sure how much was good submissive manners—or just plain old hookup manners—to say. "It didn't end well."

His heavy-lidded stare didn't change, but the sharp line of his mouth softened somewhat. "Come sit," he said, indicating the chair next to him.

"Yes, sir," I said, and something like a smile tilted his lips. He was pleased by that.

After crossing the room to the chair, I sat and smoothed the black velvet of my dress over my legs. I crossed my ankles and folded my hands in my lap, my back straight. His eyes flicked over me, lingering on where the slender ties of the dress's halter were tied in a neat bow at the nape of my neck, and then settled on my face.

"I'm Rafe," he said and held out a hand, which I took. It was large and warm and a little rough—rougher than I would have thought given the suit and watch. Maybe he was hands-on about whatever surveys he did for the EPA?

"I know," I said. I shivered a little as his thumb brushed against the back of my hand. "The bartender told me your name."

"Then you find me at a loss, because I don't know yours," he said, keeping my hand in his. It was a light grasp —I could pull free very easily if I wanted to—but I still felt the latent power in that hand, in those fingers. "But it's okay if you'd prefer not to give it, or would rather go by a pseudonym while you're here."

"Marian," I said, catching myself before I could say the

rest. He didn't need to know I was a Fitzwalter. That could complicate things, given his position at the EPA and how my family made its money. "My name is Marian."

"Marian," he said, his eyes roaming all over my face. "A lovely name."

"Thank you."

"And do you know what I am, Marian? Here in this club, I mean?"

An easy question.

"A dominant."

"And do you consider yourself a submissive?"

I laughed a little. Because I absolutely did consider myself a submissive and had since the moment I'd learned the word—but also: "Would I be here with you if I didn't?"

His jaw moved ever so slightly to the side, but the half-smile remained. "You'd be surprised."

Maybe I would be.

"Rafe?" I asked. His thumb still ghosted over the back of my hand, a restless, searching kind of touch, like he couldn't help himself.

"Yes?"

"Should we get started, then?"

He laughed then, a short laugh that huffed through him and ended with another one of those half-smiles. "That was very assertive. I feel like you're about to scold me for showing up to a meeting unprepared."

I smiled, although I was careful how much information I surrendered as I responded. "I oversee a lot of operations for the company I work for, which means a lot of meetings. A lot of scolding."

"That must be an incredible amount of responsibility," Rafe said. He let go of my hand and then leaned back in his chair, studying me. "Is that why you came here tonight? You'd like some relief from it?"

"Yes," I said. "But I also wanted this before I came into my job too. It took me some time to find the courage to seek it out."

"Because of the time it didn't end well," he stated.

"That's right."

He regarded me for a moment and then spoke. "I'd like to play with you while I'm here in Sherwood, Marian, if you're willing, but I believe we should move forward… deliberately."

In that voice, with that accent, *deliberately* sounded ironclad.

Absolute.

Knowing I probably wouldn't like the answer, I asked, "*Deliberately* means slowly, doesn't it?"

"It's purely selfish on my part," he said, putting his elbow on the arm of the chair and leaning his head against his thumb and forefinger. His suit jacket stretched across his shoulders and clung to the heavy curves of his biceps. "Your newness excites me. I want to savor it. Taste every moment of it. And I have no interest in denying myself."

The last sentence came out rougher than the ones before it, and heat pooled low in my belly in response.

"Oh," I said, on a soft exhale. "I see."

"I hope you do. Now the first thing I'll need you to do is draft a list of hard limits—the things you have no interest in trying—and then a list of 'maybe' limits. Things that aren't a *never*, but they're also a 'not right now'. And then" —his free hand flexed again as he said the next part—"I need you to tell me the things you want the most. The things you dream about having done to you, the things you would ask for every night if you had your way."

"Okay," I said, fighting not to shift in my seat. "I can—I can do that."

Rafe pulled a black card from his jacket pocket and handed it to me. His name and phone number were inked there in a small font. A matte, dark gold. "You can text your list to me tomorrow, and then we can meet again tomorrow night."

"Do *you* have any hard limits?" I asked suddenly. "Do dominants have those?"

"Of course they do, but as it happens, my own hard limits are very few. I only ask that..." He paused, as if choosing his words carefully, and then started again. "If we aren't a good fit as a dom and sub, that's perfectly all right, and we will part ways as friends. But I'm no more naturally a submissive or a switch than I am a badger or a lion, and I play best with someone who's comfortable with that very inescapable reality."

I looked at him again—this time not as a baby submissive in way over her head, but like I would a client or consultant or wayward COO. Like he was sitting in my Seattle office, staring at me from across my desk, armed to the teeth with his own unknowable corporate agenda. He was not a closed book—the barely suppressed restlessness and the smudges under his eyes betrayed too much for that —but he was also hardly easy to read.

Whether it was work, loneliness, or heartbreak that haunted him, I couldn't tell. Maybe it was none of those things. Maybe it was all of them.

"Are you asking this because it's happened before?" I asked.

He inclined his head. "You have your time when something didn't end well, and I have mine."

Curiosity pricked at my insides, but I'd had years of

practice at hiding it. "I don't think you have to worry about that with me," I reassured him. "I'm submissive to the core, and you're only here temporarily as it is. Hardly enough time for more...complicated feelings to emerge."

He made a small noise of assent and then leaned forward, as if to stand. "In that case, darling, I very much look forward to hearing from you tomorrow."

"Will we fuck?" I blurted inelegantly. "When we play?"

He laughed—a fast, rasping laugh that went away as quickly as it had come. "Do you want to fuck, Marian?"

"Yes," I said. At the very first BDSM munch I'd gone to in college, a well-meaning host had explained to me that kink didn't have to be sexual, that a scene didn't have to include sex, and that I could enjoy the catharsis and sensation of kink without bringing desire into the equation. I'd appreciated the nuance, but for better or worse, kink got me hot. I very, very much wanted my kink to be sexual.

"Then yes, Marian," Rafe replied, leaning forward and catching my hand. "We'll fuck."

"Good," I breathed, as he dropped a soft kiss to the back of my hand. His lips grazed over my knuckles, giving just a whisper of tongue. Taking just a taste.

He was tasting me.

The response that evoked in me must have been hard to miss. He dropped his eyes to the bodice of my gown, where I knew the tips of my breasts were pressing hard against the velvet, and then his gaze traced over the fresh goosebumps peppering my exposed arms.

Somehow I'd gone from thinking I wasn't ready for anything at all to burning alive with need, and the idea of leaving The Knot without *something*—without even a mark, without a hint of the mayhem I wanted Rafe to sketch on my body—was agonizing. I needed something, I needed more.

I *needed*, period.

"Can't we...can't we do something tonight?" I asked.

He lifted his head from where he'd been kissing my hand. That was contrary to another college-munch-factoid I'd learned: a dominant would never have their head lowered, they'd never perform such an obeisant deed as kissing someone's hand. And yet as Rafe looked up at me, he didn't seem diminished or any less powerful than before. He looked *pleased* that he'd kissed me and tasted my skin. Like he'd seen something he wanted and he'd taken it and now it was his.

"Please?" I added for good measure.

"It's not a good idea," he said.

"That's not a *no*."

He straightened all the way up but kept hold of my hand, the tips of his fingers resting against where the pulse thrummed in my wrist. "I can't tell if you're this used to negotiating or if you're a blossoming brat."

He didn't sound irritated—though it was hard to tell with that rough, half-growling voice—but he did sound stern. Which my body responded to immediately.

"Probably the first one, but I wouldn't discount the second," I said, a little breathlessly. "Please, Rafe. Sir."

He sighed and shook his head, as if I were nothing but trouble and he was of half a mind to do something about it. "You should have time to think this over. To consider if you'd still like to play after we've talked about limits and such. *But*," he added, forestalling the protest already on my lips, "I suppose a little something wouldn't hurt. Just a sample."

"Yes, please," I said, already moving forward. I hoped

he'd take me over his knee or order me over to the bench. Or that he'd strip off my dress and make me endure his assessing stare...

Whatever it was, I was *ready*. In the space of an hour, I'd converted from doubt to eagerness, and maybe it was only that I'd needed a push in the right direction—or maybe it was because, for the first time since my parents' death and my sudden inheritance of their empire, I found myself breathing easy and free. Here in this room, here with this man.

Here with his kiss lingering on my skin and his pale blue eyes reflecting the small fire behind me.

A noise rumbled in Rafe's throat at my eagerness. A little laugh, maybe.

"Well, then. Let's see what would be dirty enough for a prim little thing like you."

I didn't bother arguing the *prim little thing*. I'd been raised an heiress and had spent my life cloistered in boarding schools and stuffy society events. Manners and decorum had been baked into me from the beginning, which was probably why I'd developed such a girlhood fixation on Lox. She'd been born into the same world, fettered with the same expectations, and yet she'd somehow remained entirely herself, entirely her own stubborn yet playful person. The pressure that had eventually frozen me into porcelain had simply rolled off Lox the same way rain rolls off leaves in a forest.

"*Red* means stop," said Rafe. "*Yellow* means slow down."

"Will I really need a safeword for this?" I asked doubtfully.

One of those broad shoulders lifted. "Possibly not. But I don't play without them. Now get on your knees, Marian."

I obeyed as quickly as I could, my heart thumping hard

against my chest as I knelt in front of him. I reached for my dress, to arrange it better around myself, but he caught my wrist with his hand.

"No, no," he tutted, guiding me all the way upright. "I didn't ask you to make yourself look all lovely and composed. And that's because I want you *dis*composed. I want you rumpled and undone, and I want you messy, and I suppose now is as good a time as any for you to learn that I always get what I want. Always."

He pulled my wrist up to his mouth, and I breathed out at the feel of his lips on my skin once more.

"What are you going to do?" I whispered.

"Punish," he said simply, and then he bit the inside of my wrist.

Pain flashed—bright, metallic—and then died away as quickly as it had come to life. Rafe raised his face to study the indented parentheses he'd left on my pale skin, which were quickly going from a bloodless white to a dark, angry red, and then he dropped a kiss onto the same spot.

I sucked in a breath, not sure whether that kiss felt good or bad, strung between the two poles of pleasure and pain like an electric current.

"Now," he said softly, releasing my bitten wrist, "are we ready to listen?"

"Yes," I said, and then added a hasty, "*Sir*," when he lifted an eyebrow at me.

"Good," he said crisply. "I want you to kiss my shoe."

I froze.

Part of me, the executive officer part, was already scoffing. *That's all?* I wanted to ask. *That's it?* I did deeply unpleasant tasks every day, from fielding meetings with disgruntled shareholders to enduring acquisition pitches over tedious lunches—and I knew I was capable of anything for the sake of a goal. That the goal was proving myself to a dominant and not to an investor wasn't the point here. The point was that I could do it and had indeed done worse. With worse people too.

But the other part of me, the part that knew a dessert fork from an oyster fork, the part that had season tickets to the ballet and hadn't sneezed in public for twelve years, couldn't even process the command. The Bond No. 9 lipstick I was wearing had cost as much as some people earned in a day; my mouth hadn't come that close to the ground since I was child playing in Sherwood Forest, darting through the trees with Lox and Will and Tuck.

The idea of touching my mouth to Rafe's shoe, which had walked across the undoubtedly fluid-spattered floor of The Knot, which had probably walked over airport terminal carpet and through wet parking lots and God knew where else...

"You can say *red*," Rafe reminded me. His voice was neutral, devoid of inflection. "You don't have to do anything you don't want to do."

But of course, I wasn't only a CEO and a socialite—I was *Marian* too, the same person who once dreamed of having Robin Loxley pull on my hair and bite my mouth. The girl who'd dreamed about a kind of love that was bruising and dark, and raw in its exposed lust—and of course I knew this thing with Rafe de Lacy wouldn't ever be love, but it would be as close as I'd ever come to the rest of it now that Lox was gone.

Before Rafe could speak again, I braced my hands on either side of his feet and lowered myself down, going slowly, carefully. I wanted to do this right; I wanted Rafe pleased with me.

The realization was like a bloom of clarity in my mind. I wanted to please the wolf, and so nothing else mattered.

The top of Rafe de Lacy's shoe gleamed.

My wrist throbbed where he'd bitten it.

I pressed my lips to the leather and kissed his shoe.

THE FITZWALTER MANSION was perched on the rocky edge of the world, with the ocean at its front and the dark expanse of Sherwood Forest at its back. It had always been private—practically monastic—but now with my parents dead, it often felt worse than private. It felt robbed and hollow, lonely in the kind of way that only houses near the water could be lonely.

But tonight, I felt none of that. I parked in the garage and walked into the house in a kind of daze, my wrist still singing with Rafe de Lacy's punishment, and my knees still aching from his commands. My body still wound tight with hunger.

He'd rewarded the kiss on his shoe with a single, fond pet of my head, and then had helped me to my feet. "You did very well," he'd said. And after he'd studied my wrist for a moment, he'd flicked those blue eyes up to mine. "Very well, indeed, Marian."

"Thank you," I'd whispered. The place between my legs had been tight, hot, wet enough to feel on my thighs. I'd wanted him to do so much more to me, to use me and fuck me, and I'd seen the way he'd adjusted his erection as he'd stood up...

But with another soft kiss to the marks on my wrist, he'd left.

Silently, quickly, like he'd had more prey to chase after tonight.

As I stepped into the large central room of the house, I wondered if Rafe really *did* have more prey to chase. More submissives to lure in with those wide shoulders and strange eyes.

I wasn't upset by the idea, but I couldn't say I felt excited about it either. I wandered over to the floor-to-ceiling windows which looked out over the sea and watched the rain streak down into the water below, wondering if I was jealous.

With a loud click, a lamp came on behind me. I turned, stumbling back into the window, and saw a tall, fair woman with green eyes and too many freckles sitting on the sofa. She was wearing boots and cargo pants with a tank top and a sleeveless vest, the latter of which was unzipped and opened to reveal the straps of a leather shoulder harness with an empty holster. Her dark red hair was shaved close on one side and then left longish and tousled on the other.

The last time I'd seen her, her hair had been in a thick, regulation ponytail. I'd heard a few years ago that she'd had to shave it all off for Ranger school, but that was only hearsay.

She'd stopped talking to me long before then.

"Lox," I said hoarsely, the window cold against the bare skin of my back. "You're here."

She dipped her pointed chin in assent.

"But you—you can't be here."

Her lips were painted a dark, dark color, and so I saw the moment her mouth flattened. "No, little fox," she said, and I swallowed to hear the name that used to be mine, the name only she had ever called me. "I *shouldn't* be here. There is a difference, you see."

I stared at her, still hardly believing she was back in Sherwood. The stories about her—the things those FBI agents had asked me—

The way she'd just dropped me after she'd left five years ago, like I hadn't existed to her at all—

"*But*," Lox said, sitting back and propping a boot across her knee, "I heard something so fucking ridiculous that I had to come and see for myself whether it was true or not."

I processed complex information all day, every day. I'd had to learn about ocean currents and the native habitats of cork trees and the vagaries of a stock market that still favored resource exploitation over renewable technology. And yet I could not process this.

Lox.

Here.

Now.

Even the scent of her was here. Cedar and loam, the smell of the forest behind my house. Every breath I dragged in was dosed with it.

"What did you hear?" I managed to whisper.

A muscle jumped in the slender line of her jaw. "That you were at The Knot tonight. With a man named Rafe de Lacy."

TWO

LOX

For a long moment, there was only the rain on the glass, the distant churn of the sea outside. Then Marian lifted her chin.

"It's none of your business whom I kneel to," she said, her voice as cool as the room around us. "Especially after what you've done."

"It is my business when you're kneeling to Rafe de Lacy," I told her, ignoring her little dig about the things I'd done. I probably deserved it. "He's not the kind of person you should be playing with."

Marian straightened up off the glass, stepping into the pool of lamplight and allowing me to see her properly for the first time in five years.

She wasn't any taller than she'd been at eighteen, but her bearing had changed, had grown into a natural grace that made me think of old Hollywood films and present-day duchesses. Her hair—dark as the Army coffee I used to choke down before PT—was pulled back in a chignon that exposed the long lines of her throat and clavicle. It also had the effect of showing off the little bow behind her neck that held up the bodice of her dress, and abruptly all I could think about was tugging on those slender ties and watching the velvet tumble down her breasts.

But I managed not to betray myself; I kept my eyes firmly on her face. On those blue eyes fringed with thick, dark lashes, the upturned nose, that lush mouth. Her lower lip was so full that there was a small crease underneath it, and I lost myself for a moment remembering how it felt to pull that lip between my teeth and bite.

"I think it's a little rich of you to tell me who to play with," Marian said crisply. "And I would ask you how you got into my house without me knowing, but I remember enough from my interview with the FBI agents that I don't have to."

I hadn't known they'd been to see her. *Goddammit.*

"You were interviewed," I said, and somehow managed to keep my tone level. Good. She didn't need to know how close she was to the havoc I'd wreaked—and the havoc I planned to wreak still. "Why didn't you tell me?"

She crossed her arms, which only served to push her tits up higher under the velvet. A kick of desire pulsed low in my belly, but I forced myself to ignore it. I'd lived this long without touching her again, and I would probably survive the lack. Although the idea of *Rafe* touching her sent a tumult of emotion crashing through me, and I hated the thought of that amoral wolf getting to see her on her knees for him, I hated it more than I hated almost anything else in this cold, greedy world.

So why couldn't I stop imagining what it must have looked like? Marian, kneeling in a pool of dark velvet?

A suited Rafe looking on, his mouth carved in a satisfied near-smile?

"I don't know, Lox," she said, sounding exasperated now. "My parents died and I was trying to single-handedly run a corporation I had no business running. I had a lot more going on than whatever trouble you'd gotten yourself into. And if you'll recall, I had *no way to tell you*, given that you'd ghosted me years before."

"You could have told Tuck," I said. "Or Will. They would have gotten it to me."

An elegant eyebrow arched. "You still talk to them?" When I didn't answer, she sighed. "Of course you do. Of course it was only me that you cut off."

"Don't," I said. "Don't invent a story simply because you don't know the truth."

"Why don't you enlighten me then?" Marian asked. "Because we'd kissed that afternoon and then"—she flushed, presumably at the memory of what had happened after we'd kissed. But she determinedly moved past it— "you didn't return my calls, my texts, my emails. You ignored me for five years—and only me, it seems—and now you're here, telling me to stay away from Rafe de Lacy without explaining why. Or even explaining how the hell you know who Rafe de Lacy is."

She turned away, to gather herself perhaps, but it had the effect of revealing the low back of her dress to me, of revealing the length of her spine, the delicate sculpture of her shoulder blades.

The neat little bow at her nape which was all that stood between me and seeing her bared to my gaze.

Instinct took hold as I stood. She went very still as I approached, her shoulders tense, her eyes straight ahead, and I couldn't resist: I ghosted a single finger down the valley of her back. Goosebumps followed my touch like contrails streaking behind a jet engine.

"I think about the day I left all the time, little fox," I said quietly, now running the tip of my finger along the curve of her shoulder. "We said goodbye right over there by the front door. Do you remember? Because I do. I remember so well it hurts."

She didn't move, didn't look back at me, but I felt the catch in her breath. She liked knowing that I remembered. It mattered to her.

"You were wearing a yellow dress and ballet flats, and you looked like spring itself. And the shade of lipstick you wore that day...like the inside of a petal. It was smeared all over your mouth by the time I left."

"Stop it," she said, spinning on her heel to face me. Taking two large steps back. "Stop—*taunting* me."

"I'm not taunting you," I said. "I'm reminding you. You were everything to me that day, and that's why I couldn't keep you. Because that's what it would have been: *keeping*. I couldn't give you the kind of partnership of equals your parents had, I couldn't even have given you the generous affection my own parents had with each other. I wanted to have you in a way that would have meant—"

I stopped, tried again. "You weren't supposed to want it back," I attempted. "You weren't supposed to want the way we were that afternoon, not after we were done at least. You were supposed to realize that you'd been caught up in the heat of the moment and that you actually preferred someone easy to be with. Someone kind."

She stared at me. "So you ghosted me because you were afraid that you were going to...what? Taint me with kink? Is that it?"

It sounded so ridiculous when she put it like that. But

she couldn't have seen herself that day, with her hair all disheveled and her dress wrinkled from kneeling on the floor. She couldn't have known what I wanted to do to her then, how much I wanted to pin her to the floor and ruin her for anyone else, anyone else ever.

"I left you alone because I am not *safe* for you," I said sharply. "And that became truer and truer as the years went on."

The doubt was sketched all over her face. "Really."

"Yes. Really. You weren't interviewed by federal agents because I've been leading a quiet life, you know."

"And I suppose you're not going to tell me anything about this unquiet life?"

The wind picked up outside, flinging the rain against the glass walls of the house. I imagined that I could hear the forest on the other side of the road, all wild and tossing in the storm, and I closed my eyes. No matter where I'd gone—as the Loxley heir, as a soldier, as a spy—Sherwood had always been home. Had always been the plan.

"It's not a good idea," I said after a minute, opening my eyes. "I'm being looked for as we speak. The less you know about what I'm doing, the better."

"But you seem to know plenty about what I'm doing," she said. She watched me as I took a step closer, and then another step, the fall of my boots barely audible over the rain. "You knew where I was tonight, and with whom."

"Much Miller was at The Knot tonight," I said. I was close enough to touch her now, but I didn't. "He saw you."

"Tuck's friend," she said to herself and then shook her head. "I didn't know he was back in Sherwood."

I didn't tell her that he'd only recently returned, along with me and Jovanna. Even showing myself to Marian tonight was a risk, given that Rafe was already here and no doubt looking for me, but he'd left me no choice. "He saw you and Rafe. And Marian...I'll grant that I might have been wrong about you and kink, but I'm not wrong about Rafe. He's a dangerous man, and he absolutely cannot be trusted. He is ruthless, merciless. He doesn't feel things like the rest of us do."

Marian's hand went to her wrist as I spoke, and then she quickly dropped it, like she'd given away a secret. But it was too late anyway. Those wine-colored crescents were the first thing I'd noticed as she'd wandered dazedly into the house.

A Rafe de Lacy signature if I ever saw one.

"Would he hurt me during a scene?" Marian asked. "Ignore a safeword?"

"No," I said, reaching now for her bruised wrist. I wrapped my fingers around it, the slender bones nestling perfectly into my palm, and I lifted it up so I could study the marks more closely. They were deep enough that they would properly bruise, but despite the small starbursts of broken blood vessels, the skin itself wasn't split. It took more care than one might think to bite a lover like this, to ensure a bite's memory without drawing blood. "Rafe is generally very careful about his kink."

Except with me, I wanted to add, but I didn't. I couldn't lay the brutal frenzy that had been between us at his feet.

Or not *entirely* at his feet, at least.

"Then I don't see a problem," Marian said flatly. "If he's not going to harm me—"

"I didn't say he wasn't going to harm you," I cut in. "I said he wasn't going to violate the space of a scene. Those are two different things. And," I added, running my thumb over the marks on her wrist, "I still can't promise that he wouldn't use kink to further his own ends, even if he's still technically within the bounds of what's safe."

Marian didn't pull herself free, but she did give me an impatient look. "If he's not going to hurt me during play, then this concern is pointless, because he and I won't be together otherwise. He's not proposing marriage; he's not trying to...I don't know, invest in my company or wedge himself into my daily life or something. And as for furthering his own ends, what exactly *are* those ends, Lox? Do they have anything to do with how you know him?"

Yes, was what I should have said. *He's looking for me. He'll use you to find me.*

I found myself hesitating to say it, though. Hesitating when I never hesitated, when I did everything quickly, intuitively, without worrying about what would come next. But this was *Marian*; this was my little fox. If I fucked up with myself, if I fucked up with Will and Jovanna and the others who'd elected to join me, then at least we'd chosen this chaotic path with our eyes wide open. But Marian Fitzwalter had nothing to do with our missions and our treasons. She had nothing to do with the NSA or the Castle of the North Wind.

It should stay that way.

"Rafe and I were together," was what I finally landed on. It was the truth, even if it wasn't the whole truth. "A while back. It didn't end well."

Lying like this went against all the principles I had about what people deserved to know about their own lives, their own decisions. But ironically enough, the closer someone was to me, the less I gave a shit about what I believed.

Maybe Rafe had been right about me all along. Maybe I was something worse than a thief: a faithless liar.

Marian's pretty mouth flattened into an unimpressed line. "So that's it then. You've come to warn me off your ex-lover."

I knew how it sounded. I knew how it must seem. But while I could pull up stakes and vanish at a moment's notice, Marian could not. She was tied to Sherwood and to her family's company, and that would make her easy to find and easy to interrogate.

Maybe even easy to arrest.

And I had to assume that Rafe would use every trick he knew to flush me out of hiding.

"Please," I said. "Please just stay away from him. He's up to no good, Marian, I know it."

"You think an awful lot of yourself if you think that he'd play with me just to hurt you."

Not just to hurt me, little fox. He's playing with you because I'm wanted for treason, and it's his job to bring me in.

"You already know I think a lot of myself," I said instead, and I did have to smile at the face she made. "But I'm still right."

Marian looked down to where I held her wrist. The tips of my fingers rested along the delicate tendons there, just above the blue threads of her veins. If someone walked in and saw us like this, it might look like I was holding her in place. It might look like

I was showing her that I didn't need padded cuffs or bondage rope to have command over her.

She looked back up to me, blue eyes soft in the lamp-light, and I knew she was thinking the same thing.

"Did he bite you anywhere else?" I murmured, suddenly wanting to know. Wanting to see. "Did he untie that little dress and then bite all the pretty skin he found there?"

Her throat moved in a small swallow. "No," she murmured. "He said we had to discuss limits before we played. We only—we only did one small thing."

She was flushing again, and I burned to know, the jealousy like fire in my veins.

"What did you do?" I asked, knowing I had no right to ask and doing it anyway.

And strangely enough, Marian didn't seem to care either. Her skin was pebbled with goosebumps, her pulse thrumming in her throat. Her eyes when they met mine looked drugged.

I wondered if she'd let me pull her even closer. Close enough for me to run my nose along her cheek, over the hollow of her temple.

"I kissed his shoe," she said, a little unsteadily. "Only that."

"Only that?" That was enough, as far as I was concerned. On par with canes and climaxes. Practically a collar. "Did you like it?"

Her cheeks were stained a deep red now, along with her chest. I wanted to lick those stains. I wanted to know if they felt as warm as they looked.

"Yes," she admitted in a whisper.

Our faces had come close without my meaning for them to, close enough that I could feel her breath on my lips. I was only a few inches taller than her, but it was enough of a difference that I would need to angle my head just right if I wanted to kiss her...

"Lox," she said, in a voice that barely carried over the rain. "I'd do it for you too, you know. If you'd let me. I'd kiss your feet, I'd get on my knees for you, and it could be like it was that afternoon. Just like that."

I swayed toward her—her wrist still in my hand, my other hand reaching up to palm that pretty little chignon— but then a growl of thunder rolled through the house and I suddenly remembered where I was.

Sherwood, where the trees met the sea.

Sherwood, where Marian needed to stay, and stay without any connection to me.

I let go of her wrist and took a few steps backward. She blinked at me, dazed and bereft.

"Lox?" she murmured.

"I have to go," I said, fighting the urge to stalk back over to her and finish what we'd started. To sear away her memory of Rafe's touch. "I'm sorry."

"But—"

"I know this probably goes without saying, but it would be best if you didn't mention to anyone that you saw me. Even Rafe." *Especially Rafe.*

"Am I going to see you again?" she asked quietly, and framed in the rain like this, clad in velvet and begging to be handled, she was eerily like the dreams I used to have of her when I was still inside that NSA nightmare of a life. When I was so deep in hell that the only sleep I got were half hour snatches in broad daylight while Rafe kept watch.

"I don't know," I told her honestly. "I shouldn't even be here now. It's not a good idea for me to stay in one place long."

"I see," she said. She turned back to the window, wrapping her arms around herself. "Then take care, Lox. I hope the hiding goes well."

I didn't like hearing the bitterness in her voice, but what could I do? Implicate her in treason because I wanted to kiss her so badly it hurt?

"Goodbye, Marian," I said, and with my jaw clenched from the effort it took, I left her alone.

Alone with the rain and the dark half-moons Rafe de Lacy had left on her wrist.

RAFE

THEY CALLED it The Castle of the North Wind, but most people would call it what it was: a den of thieves.

And it was here in Sherwood. I was certain of it.

I was walking on a well-maintained but deeply soggy trail through the trees, having eschewed my usual suit for boots, jeans, and a worn flannel shirt—the uniform of someone in the area for boring ecology reasons and nothing else.

Out of the fog emerged the shape of a man bent over a paper map, and he looked up as I approached. He was also in jeans and flannel, although with his septum piercing, clear-framed glasses, and black hair tied back in a bun, he looked more PNW Hipster than Forgettable EPA Employee.

Which made sense, since today Joshua Zhang wasn't dressed as anyone other than himself.

As I passed him, my old friend folded the map into neat rectangles and fell in step beside me. The trail was deserted, and foggy as hell besides, and so there was little need for the usual precautions that accompanied such meetings.

"Thanks for coming," I said to Joshua, still discreetly scanning the periphery as we walked north toward the scenic overlook just a half mile or so from here. We obviously wouldn't be able to see anything in this weather, but it was always better to have a destination during a rendezvous on foot. It lent verisimilitude to whatever pretense you were meeting under, and it kept you moving.

Always better to keep moving.

"You know us CISA types like to meet in an office, right?" Joshua asked. "Hell, even the NSA knows how to use a phone."

"Did you really want to have a conversation about how a CIA operative is running a mission on American soil on behalf of the NSA over the phone?"

Joshua heaved a sigh. "I guess not, when you put it like that, given that it's a *tad* on the illegal side. Technically, at least. Also you can stop casing the literal trees. No one's hiding in this wet-ass forest."

I opened my mouth, but he flapped the folded map at me. "Don't start telling me some story about the one time people *were* hiding in a forest, because no one cares, you SOG bastard. How's the search going?"

I glanced around the trees again. Nothing but moss and mushrooms and exposed hemlock roots like plump, raised veins. "I found the girl."

"Mark's information was good?"

Ferns rustled against me as I walked along the edge of the path to give Joshua enough room to skirt a puddle. "It's always good, Joshua. It's the price that's the problem."

I could feel his gaze sliding over to me. "Do I want to know what the price was?"

"Probably not." Even *I* wished I could unknow the information I'd given Mark Trevena in exchange for the details he knew about the girl who'd once stolen Lox's heart here in Sherwood. But what was done was done.

"I don't like working with him," Joshua muttered as we passed a fallen spruce. Its dead trunk was massive enough that new trees were growing on top of it, their roots draping over the moss-covered sides of the log like ribbons. "I don't trust him."

"I don't either." Of all the people I'd met in my life—both as a Green Beret and as a CIA officer—Mark Trevena was one of the few who truly scared me. "But he's a necessary evil."

"He's the devil," Joshua muttered. "The devil in a good suit. And with a BDSM club."

That BDSM club—called Lyonesse and nestled in the heart of Washington DC—was precisely the reason why Mark had the information he did, but Joshua already knew that, so I didn't bother to point it out.

"I just don't know if it's a good idea to involve him in anything," Joshua went on. We were close to the scenic overlook now, our boots crunching over the wet gravel as we approached where the trail skirted against the lip of a steep green valley. A quick-moving stream at the bottom sparkled through the fog. "Surely, we can get what we need from SIGINT."

SIGINT—or signal intelligence—was data intelligence agencies pulled from things like emails, texts, phone calls—and even from unmanned aerial vehicles equipped with Lidar and Radar sensors. This was opposed to human intelligence gathered from people: assets, allies, and captured enemies alike. Joshua, as a former NSA mathematician and current Assistant Regional Director of the newish Cybersecurity & Infrastructure Security Agency—and whose entire world was computers and cryptography and data—obviously preferred SIGINT.

As an officer of the Special Operations Group—the paramilitary arm of the CIA—I had a partiality for human intelligence. As did Mark Trevena.

"Signal intelligence only gets us so far," I said, coming to a stop at the overlook's damp wooden railing. "And John Lackland himself approved using Mark, you know."

Joshua snorted. "Lackland is a brainless jackass and you know it."

I did know it. Lackland was the deputy director of the NSA—a position he came into via combination of nepotism and better candidates getting pulled elsewhere—and he'd done nothing during his tenure but sow distrust and make ethically dicey choices. Ethically dicey choices that were still deemed okay by the powers that be, but when those choices were made by design to be plausibly deniable *by* the powers that be, that approval didn't mean very much.

Still, he was the boss. And while I was on loan from the CIA to the NSA, he was *my* boss.

"At least we all have the same goal," Joshua said, flicking away the raindrops that had accumulated on his map. "And I don't think anyone wants to find Lox more than the three of us."

No one wanted to find Lox more than *me*, but Zhang didn't know about the twisted romance Lox and I had once shared, and I'd rather keep it that way. It was only because Lox and I once had an official working relationship via joint intelligence missions that I'd been tapped to help find her now.

Only I knew exactly how personal this mission was to me.

"I can't believe I never saw this coming," Joshua said. "Three years on the same team with her, and I had no idea."

Neither had I, and Lox and I had been a lot more than teammates. The American government had gone from having one of the world's best cryptographers to having that cryptographer actively stealing some very important secrets from government databases.

And to what end still remained an utter mystery. She hadn't sold any information to any of our usual enemies— at least that we knew about—and she hadn't made any of it public through the press.

She hadn't done anything, actually, other than go into hiding and continue to steal things that definitely did not belong to her.

"But hey, you're the best operative in the CIA—or at least you are now that Mark Trevena left to start a spanking club or whatever," added Joshua. "If anyone can find Lox, you can. With our help, of course."

"Right," I said, bracing my elbows on the railing and trying to make out the trees on the other side of the misty divide. "Tell me what we've got."

"We've got three CISA specialists and two NSA agents arriving tomorrow. They'll be bouncing between the safe-house here in Sherwood and our temporary headquarters in Olympia, where we'll be housing anyone else who wants to join the Lox-hunt. You'll have all the big imaging and listening toys, too; Lackland basically wrote us a blank check when it came to this mission. I just hope you're right about Lox coming back here." Joshua pulled off his glasses and ran his sleeve over his pale gold features, which were now thoroughly damp and misted.

"If I were Lox," he went on, "I'd be in a country without any extradition laws. Or up in the Yukon or something, where no one could find me and I wouldn't need any extra energy to cool down my rigs."

Cooling. Rigs. Right. "So she will need to keep her machines cooled here?" I asked, already knowing the answer. The kind of encrypted information Lox was stealing required more than a laptop to intercept, decode, and store—it needed the kind of hashing power that only came from a warehouse full of CPUs and GPUs. A warehouse that would generate a lot of heat. "We'll need thermal imaging of the area to start."

"Already put in the order for it," said Joshua. "But we should do the entire peninsula, just to be thorough.

"Good idea," I murmured, even though I privately thought it would be unnecessary. Lox was here in Sherwood. I was certain of it. "And we should be looking for people in the woods when they shouldn't be—in the middle of the night, alone. Maybe small vehicles too, but I'd imagine they'd be *very* small. Tell the imaging people to think ATVs, not trucks."

"Makes sense," Joshua said. "So we'll start with thermal. And then there's the girl, which you'll deal with."

"I'm building rapport now," I said, looking down at my hands. Hands that would be tangled in Marian Fitzwalter's hair tonight. Joshua and the team didn't know *how* I'd be building rapport—neither did the higher-ups at the NSA or the CIA. Frankly, my bosses had never cared how I'd gotten things done, as long as they'd gotten done in the end.

Well, done and with no one getting hauled in front of the Senate afterward.

Joshua made a noise that I could easily interpret as a SIGINT fan wanting to explain to me that HUMINT was too slow, too risky, and never as useful, but blessedly, he seemed more ready to leave than to sermonize.

He straightened up and tapped me on the shoulder with the map. "Secure lines will be in place at the safehouse by tonight, so next time, let's skip the mist and mushrooms and do a call?"

A call...

"Do you think it's possible Lox can hack the safehouse's comms?" I asked. I understood enough about cryptography and cybersecurity to be good at my job, but my job was patently not cryptography and cybersecurity. It was doing dangerous things in dangerous places while not getting killed by dangerous people. When it came to what exactly Lox could do and how, Joshua was the expert.

He pushed up his glasses, looking not at the valley, but at some point just beyond it, his mouth in an uncharacteristically serious line. "I don't know," he said thoughtfully. "It's possible. The best hope we have is moving fast. Before she can figure out where we are and what we have, protocol-wise."

I nodded.

"But until then, let's hope for the best, eh?"

I gave him a dubious look. "Are you in intelligence or what?" I asked. "We only exist to plan for the worst."

"I thought you only existed to kill people and look good while doing it."

"You're thinking of Mark Trevena. I haven't killed anyone." That Joshua knew of, at least.

"Right," Joshua said with a roll of his eyes, already turning to leave. "I'm still making sure I never end up on your bad side, not matter how broodily handsome it is. Talk to you soon—and emphasis on *talk*, Rafe. No more hikes through vampire territory."

I waved him away and then turned back toward the valley after he'd disappeared into the fog. I stared through the haze at the stream trilling its way down the hills and considered everything that needed to be done.

Aerial surveys, visual and thermal. Foot surveys of the forest and the town. Building enough rapport with members of The Knot to start asking about Lox, if she'd been there, if she'd been seen in Sherwood recently. Building enough rapport with Marian to do the same...

Marian.

I let out a long breath.

She was supposed to be the easiest part of this—the part that I could do in my sleep. But I hadn't planned on her being so tempting, so wonderfully, sweetly pliant. Probably because I hadn't planned on the right version of Marian to begin with.

After I'd learned from Mark that I might be able to find her at The Knot, the plan had been to lie in wait, and then offer her a drink and chat dominant to dominant. Slowly loosen her up until I could start picking at the edges of what she knew about Lox.

But then it turned out that the woman who'd managed to fuck with Robin Loxley's head—when even death and combat could barely do that—wasn't a dominant at all.

And when I walked into the club and saw her sitting alone at the bar, looking somehow vulnerable and poised at the same time, I found myself feeling something I hadn't felt since Lox left me a year ago.

Need.

Not the mindless biology of flesh seeking release, not the idle fantasies and arousals that drifted through the mind over the course of an ordinary day, but the kind of need which could bleed the world dry, which whetted my appetite even as it scorched my bones.

I myself hadn't even been sure what I planned on doing

when Marian followed me to that private room. Perhaps I really had meant to talk to her—and only talk. Perhaps I'd thought that I could somehow thread the needle between a kink-infused interaction and kink in truth.

Whatever I'd thought, it had died away the moment she'd stepped into the room.

I'm not sure what to do next, she'd admitted shyly. *If I should stand or sit or kneel...*

I'd forgotten, hadn't I, that rush of power and that roll of lust. That burn of satisfaction. The way it felt like nothing else, nothing else at all.

And with Marian, there'd been something else alongside the burn, thrumming through me tender and raw as I'd pressed my lips to her wrist and as I'd praised her obedience. It had curled in my chest as I'd fallen asleep last night and unfurled behind my ribs the moment I'd opened my eyes this morning.

The CEO with lips so full that the lower one creased right in the middle. A spine of steel, and eyes softer than a spring morning sky.

Marian Fitzwalter, the girl who'd haunted the unhauntable Lox.

I was dangerously close to becoming obsessed myself.

I gave Joshua plenty of time to leave the forest, and then I followed the trail out, feeling my phone shiver in my pocket once I reached the parking lot and decent reception again. I pulled it out to see a text message from my new asset, my new fascination.

Marian: I have my list ready. May I send it?

Three dots appeared, flashing for a second before the next message.

Marian: Sir?

The pleasure that ripped through me when I saw that word was vicious, delicious. Unwise.

I didn't care.

I got in my car, searched for some semblance of control, and then opened Marian's message to answer.

Me: Send away.

FOUR

MARIAN

THE MIST WAS PRESSING in around Sherwood, filling the spaces between trees and veiling the brick-fronted store-fronts of Sherwood's venerable downtown. The Knot itself, perched on a jut of cliff just a few minutes outside of the city limits, was barely visible in the silver gloom, and that gloom clung to my skin and hair as I parked my car and strode to the tall wooden doors which fronted the club.

I was nervous; I couldn't deny that. This was a threshold that I'd wanted to cross for years, but awful doubts were swirling around my feet along with the mist, and I couldn't seem to shake them.

It's Lox, I told myself. She'd fucked with my head by showing up last night, dredging up hurts and lusts that I thought were thoroughly sunk and rusted through. Dredging up feelings that were more dangerous than hurt and lust combined.

I wondered, as I opened the door and was welcomed inside the club, what she'd think of me if she saw me right now. I'd picked a white gown with long sleeves, sheer enough to reveal the delicate silk underthings I was wearing underneath: bra, panties, garters and garter belt, all in a soft pink. I'd woven my hair into a loose braid which was now draped over my shoulder, ready to be undone and tangled at a moment's notice, and my makeup was simple, subtle. A brush of pink gloss and then enough mascara that it would run if I were made to cry.

I'd dressed with Lox in mind as much as Rafe—which was ridiculous, because she obviously wouldn't be here. But I couldn't stop imagining her reaction to me dressed like this. Like a bride.

Or a sacrifice.

I stopped outside the doors, trying to shake loose the memory of Lox tracing over Rafe's marks with her long, slender finger. Trying to forget how it felt—for one beautiful instant—like she was about to kiss me. I wanted to cross this threshold thinking only of Rafe, only about tonight, because while I didn't feel like I owed him much as a temporary scene partner, I felt like I owed him that at least: my attention, in its fullness.

I shouldn't step into his space with my mind twisted up in thoughts of Lox. I shouldn't be connecting the two of them at all. And yet.

As fucked up as it was, it excited me a little. The idea of Lox's jealousy if she found out. The thought of fucking someone Lox had fucked.

As some kind of revenge for her leaving Sherwood, maybe? As some sort of sick way of sharing something with her?

Or maybe it felt like the final swing of the axe—the definitive drop of the guillotine between her and me. If I did this, then I would push her away before she found a way to reject me again, and there was something perversely satisfying about that.

WHEN I FINALLY WALKED INTO The Knot, I was greeted at the front by a slender, corseted person with pearly skin, long hair, and a silver collar around their throat.

"Mr. de Lacy has requested that you join him in the castle room," Caliber said, extending a hand to escort me inside, and together we walked through the beamed central hall of the club and up the stairs to a metal walkway which traversed the open air above the hall like a drawbridge over a moat.

And just like a drawbridge ultimately led to its castle gates, the walkway led to a suspended glass cube which comprised the castle room.

Our footsteps echoed on the metal as we went, and I could feel the eyes of the people in the space below us drawn up to us. The floor of the cube was solid, but with its glass walls, guests downstairs would be able to see glimpses and slices of Rafe and me as we played. In fact, I could see a slice of Rafe now as the employee led me to the door of the cube, wearing a suit that hugged the lean lines of his body to perfection.

He was currently pacing the length of the cube, not methodically, but restlessly, his eyes searching the room below, his hand raking through his hair at intervals. When the employee opened the door, he turned toward us, but I sensed he'd already heard us coming, or seen us, because he didn't seem surprised at our entrance. Although the way his eyes burned over me as he took in my sheer white dress and practically bridal underthings told me that I had surprised him there.

"Thank you, Caliber," he told the club employee, and Caliber gave an efficient but flawlessly submissive curtsey, and left us alone in the room, shutting the door behind them.

"You came tonight," said Rafe after a moment.

"You're surprised?"

"Come here, Marian," he said, not answering my question. "Please."

I came, crossing the small room over to where he'd stopped near the glass. The windows lining the hall outside the room and the reddish lights of the club combined to make the cube a place of refractions and visual echoes; it was hard to tell where the castle room ended and where it began.

The only thing that was real and solid was the suited wolf in front of me, his eyes pale and his mouth in a firm line. When I reached him, he pressed a large hand above my left breast.

I could feel my nerve-wracked heart pounding against it.

"Yes," he finally said. "I am surprised."

We stood there like that, him with his hand over my heart, our eyes locked in a world of red glimmers and soft shadows. "I told you I would come," I said quietly, because I had when we'd texted earlier today. I'd given him a thorough list—limits, soft limits, desires that made me flush to type—and he'd thanked me for my courage. Then he told me what to expect while we played together and how a scene would unfold. Unless I said *red*, I was his to do with as he pleased. If I said *yellow*, we'd slow down or pause as the situation warranted. In case my mouth was otherwise occupied, I'd be given hand signals to use for safety. Everything else was up for negotiation, except for two more absolutes: I would submit to aftercare and I would always answer honestly when he asked me a question.

"You did tell me," allowed Rafe. "But there was a reason it took you five years to come to a place like this. To find someone like me. I think that reason must have been a good one."

He didn't turn the statement into a question, and for that I was grateful, because it meant I didn't have to answer. And I was afraid that if I answered, I would tell him about Lox, and I was scared that if I told him about Lox, I would start asking questions of my own. *How did you meet? How long were you together? How did it end, and why did that ending send Lox all this way to warn me away from you?*

I didn't want to ask those questions. I couldn't. Because even if I burned to know the answers, I could never unknow them once I did, and I wasn't ready for that.

Like any victim of unrequited love, I wasn't ready to hear how Lox had found someone else, someone better, once upon a time. It was easier to pretend she hadn't, that she was a bad dream I'd only barely begun to wake from.

When I didn't speak, Rafe's mouth curled, as if he'd expected my silence. "You remember the rules?" he asked, dropping his hand.

"Yes, sir."

"Good. You look very pretty tonight."

"Thank you, sir."

"Is it for me?"

And for the girl I grew up loving, who once left me kneeling alone on the floor with lipstick smeared all over my face.

I said, carefully, "You were a consideration. Sir."

A rasping laugh. "I can't tell if you're tempting me or teasing me with these walls of yours. But we'll let it lie for now."

I must have made some kind of expression, because he asked, "Does the *for now* make you nervous, Marian?"

I had to respond honestly, and so I said, "It does."

He nodded, as if that was the answer he'd expected, and his hand went up to finger the end of my braid.

"May I ask *you* a question? Sir?"

I could feel the brush of his fingertips over the fabric of my dress as he toyed with my hair. "You may."

"Why do you care what's behind any walls of mine? We don't know each other, we haven't promised anything to each other. This is just a temporary arrangement until your work in Sherwood is done. Does it matter what I'm feeling? Or thinking? Or what baggage I might have?"

"It matters," he said, trailing his fingers up to my collarbone and neck, and from there to my chin so he could lift my face to his, "because *temporary* is not mutually exclusive with *important*. Because I want our time together to be memorable and delicious, and that only comes with surrender—not the facile surrender of a casual encounter, but the broken, bruised kind of defeat that comes with having opened yourself. I'm not asking for your life story, but I do want inside you, I do crave your breaking, and so it's important I know if these walls are because of bad kink or a bad dominant. I want to hurt you, darling—I have no desire to harm you. This is important to me."

Is it?

The question flashed through my mind almost against my will, tied to the memory of Lox in my house last night, her lips painted as dark as the rainy night outside.

I didn't say he wasn't going to harm you.

I pushed the doubt away. I didn't need Lox fucking with

my head more than she already had. If I'd decided to be here, then I was deciding to trust Rafe. Simple as that.

"It's not because of bad kink," I told him now. I didn't want him worrying about that. *No* kink at all with Lox had been the actual problem. "Or a bad dominant. And do you really crave my breaking?" I added curiously.

He laughed again, a real one that shook his body and filled the room. When he laughed like this, his entire face was transformed, and I was startled by how handsome he was. He'd been good-looking before, of course, but with that wide, boyish grin and the faintly etched lines fanning from the corners of his eyes, he was utterly arresting. The kind of man you'd stop on the street to look at. The kind of man you'd throw away your dignity to hear even one word from.

"Up on the spanking bench, sweet one," he said, still smiling. He didn't answer my question, because he didn't have to.

The command was its own answer.

I obeyed him willingly—feeling nervousness chased with excitement chased with something I couldn't entirely name but that was as close to *rightness* as I'd ever felt in my life—and knelt on the padded leather bench, making sure to kneel so that my dress could be shoved up around my waist whenever he wanted.

"Normally," Rafe said as he approached the bench, "I'd have you strip for me. I'd enjoy it, and I think you would too, given what you told me earlier today and where we are in the club."

He was right. Exhibitionism was very high on my list of desires, as was being shared, and up here in the castle, I'd be on display to the entire club.

I shivered at the thought.

"But what you're wearing tonight..." His palm skated up my thigh to my ass, lingering over the garters before following them up to the belt around my waist. "I enjoy it very much. And I suppose it would be best for us to start slowly anyway."

His hand found the ridge of my spine and stalked it up to the spot between my shoulder blades, where he slowly but inexorably pushed me down so that my stomach and chest were flat against the rest of the spanking bench.

The sheer fabric of the dress teased me with every waft of air and stir of movement as he left the bench and strolled over to a rack of floggers and paddles. With my head turned to the side, I could see the lines of his arm and torso as he touched one thing, and then another, and finally selected something with as much surety of motion as a master sculptor reaching for a certain chisel, or a painter reaching for the right brush. When he walked back to me, I saw what it was. A wide paddle, the flat part covered in a bright purple fur.

Fur.

It looked like a joke, a gag gift. Like something made for tickling. I knew there were people into kinky tickling, but *still.*

"What do you say if it gets to be too much, sweet one?" Rafe asked, stroking the paddle over the back of my exposed calf. It *did* tickle a little, but in a good way, and I felt the concurrent swells of relief and disappointment.

"Red," I replied, trying to remind myself that it would be good to go easy at first. Not that Lox had gone easy on me, that afternoon. She hadn't had a spanking bench or a rack of toys or anything other than the force of her want, and she hadn't needed it. She'd ruined me with nothing more than her bare hands in my hair.

"We'll start with ten, I think," he said as he gently—almost reverently—lifted the skirt of my dress and draped it over my ass. The fur paddle dangled by my face, as soft and fuzzy as a teddy bear. "And remember that you can use your *yellow* whenever you need."

"I don't think that will be a problem," I mumbled without thinking, and then Rafe made a noise that was very tut-tut-y and British.

"Cheeky girl," he said, but he didn't sound irritated or offended. He sounded *amused*. He sounded like he was already having a great time.

The first swat came with no warning, and it was as mild as I'd expected it to be. Still Rafe paused and ran his hand over my ass, as if consoling me, checking in on me. And then the fuzzy paddle hit again, over the spot where my panties covered my skin, and it still felt like being spanked with a doll's pillow. But again he paused, again he caressed me.

And then another swat—pause, check—and then another.

It should have been silly—and maybe it still was—but it began to feel soothing after the third or fourth swat, like being patted to sleep, and his calloused hands over my skin felt...incredible. Wonderful. Warm and large, leaving goose-bumps in their wake.

And slowly, gradually, they began to caress not only the spots the paddle had struck, but the outside of my hips, the lines of the garter belt around my waist. Everywhere but where I was beginning to need him the most.

"Ten," counted Rafe after the last one. "How are you doing, sweet one? Do you need a break?"

It would have been rude to laugh, so I didn't. But I did say, "I'm doing fine, sir. Let's keep going."

"As you wish," he said, and I heard him lift his arm behind me for another swat.

Crack.

The paddle came down like a star crashing to Earth, burning and cracking its way across my backside as it landed, and a yelp tore out of my throat as I arched off the bench, my hands flying to cover my ass.

Just like before, Rafe paused, his hand running soothingly over my skin. "Still doing okay?" he asked, and there was no hiding the amusement in his voice now. He sounded like he was very close to laughing.

He turned the handle of the paddle so that I could see the side he'd just hit me with. Instead of fur, this side was made of something flat and rubbery looking. "Silicone," he explained. "Very stingy. Makes a nice noise."

I twisted so I could glare at him. "You tricked me."

"I did," he said, not sounding the least bit sorry. "It was very fun."

And the way he was right now, with the excitement in his eyes and the smile like he'd just discovered a secret game no one else had ever played before, he reminded me so much of Lox that it hurt. However it'd happened, it made a strange kind of sense that they would've been drawn together.

It also made sense that it wouldn't have lasted.

You have your time when something didn't end well, and I have mine.

"Now," Rafe said, "would you like a break? Would you like to stop?"

I could say *red* now. I could even say *yellow*, easy yellow, safer than a safeword even, because it wouldn't break a scene, wouldn't stop any games or end any nights.

But by now the paddle's burn had settled deep inside

my skin, and there was an answering heat in my body, as if the temperature of my blood itself had changed. That sense of rightness from earlier returned, carried on wings of adrenaline and dopamine.

"No, sir," I said. "I don't want to stop."

"Then back over the bench, sweet one. Let's do ten more of these, shall we?"

Ten?!

What had sounded like a laughable number just a few minutes ago sounded impossible now. Like torture. One swat alone had stunned me—

Crack.

The paddle came down harder than the first time, searing the skin where it struck on the outside of my panties, and merely hurting like hell where it struck *over* my panties. I managed to stay on the bench, but the noise that left my body was impossible to swallow. A moan that turned soft and breathless when Rafe rubbed a hand over the skin he'd just punished, sending sparks flying everywhere through my body. The pain was already mostly gone, and there was a tightness in my belly now, a kindled desire that made me want to shift my hips so that Rafe would rub me elsewhere.

And then another crack came, loud and hard, and then more rubbing. This time the pain lingered a bit longer, fire on my skin and sinking deep into my muscles, and I was so, so aware of the fabric of the dress around my hips, of my silk panties growing wet over my pussy, of the garters that interrupted the paddle's bite every time it landed.

The next three times hurt enough to make me cry out, and the three times after that were a blur of pain and pleasure as Rafe's hands soothed away the sting and began moving closer and closer to my cunt as he stroked me.

The penultimate strike was what pushed me to the edge, though. It landed right between my bottom and my thigh with a crack loud enough to fill the room.

I let out a choked noise as tears burned my eyelids, but for the first time, Rafe's hands trailed over my silk-covered cunt, pressing and teasing and making me arch to seek more of his touch even as tears spilled down my cheeks. It hurt so bad and it felt so *good*—I was on fire, but it was the fire of stars and wishes and lust itself—and I wanted more, I needed more, more pain, more touching, more *him*—

The final swing of the paddle, and I was crying for real now, my tears coming fast and hard and my body moving on the spanking bench before I even understood what I was truly doing. I only became aware of it as Rafe dropped the paddle on the floor and *tsk*ed at me.

"Such a needy pet," he said, sounding like he was shaking his head. He grabbed my hips with both hands and pulled me back on the bench, his hands already sliding into my panties before I'd found my balance. "If you need it so badly that you're grinding against the bench, then I suppose I'd better give it to you."

My eyes fluttered closed at the first slide of his fingers against my bare, slick skin, and then I heard a deep noise of want spill from one of us.

It was him.

"You feel," he said, sounding unsteady for the first time tonight, "like nothing else."

His fingers found my clit, his other hand found my entrance. With an expertise that bordered on criminal, he began working my wet cunt open, softly strumming my clitoris all the while.

I'd never been fast at orgasming, not even alone with myself, but within a single minute, I felt the climax knotting itself fast and hard around my womb, responding helplessly to the clever fingers currently pleasuring me.

"Rafe," I breathed, the orgasm drawing agonizingly close. "Sir. Sir. Sir."

"Hold still, darling," he said, because I was a restless thing on the bench, wanting more and more and more. "Let me give you your prize. I'd hate to have to tie you up," he added, not sounding like he'd hate it at all.

In fact, it was that very thought that sent me over the edge. With the thought of Rafe's flashing eyes as he tied me to a bed, I tumbled straight into gorgeous oblivion. Everything from my navel to my knees surged and clenched and crested into a wave of sensation so powerful I could hardly stand it. And when Rafe slid his fingers free and shoved them in my mouth, my orgasm redoubled itself, began anew, driven by the pain lingering on my skin and by his fingers on my clit and by his fingers in my mouth and his mesmerizing eyes and his greedy amusement and him him *him*—

"I hope I'm not interrupting anything," a woman's voice said from across the room.

My orgasm receded as I turned my head to look, but Rafe didn't pull his hand free of my panties, nor did he slide his fingers from my mouth. He kept fingering me as the woman approached from the door, striding in with knee-high boots, tight black pants, and a cropped leather jacket still spotted with rain. A motorcycle helmet hung from her right hand.

"*Lox*," I breathed around Rafe's fingers, at the same time he said, in a voice that was utterly devoid of emotion, "Lox. Welcome."

LOX

Of the things I regretted most in my life—and they were many—I most regretted never seeing Marian Fitzwalter come. I especially regretted it now, having seen her gasp and arch at Rafe's skilled touch, watching her fall apart under someone else's care, knowing that it wasn't my hand inside her designer panties, knowing that it wasn't my welts on her backside that had driven her to the point of madness.

I had once shoved my fingers in her mouth though. That I had done before the Tom Ford-clad monster in front of me had, and I couldn't help feeling a little smug about it.

As for the pulse of swollen need currently making my entire cunt throb, I tried my best to ignore it. It was only because Marian was bent over in that white dress like a bride bent over an altar. It was only because I'd just seen her lips part in mindless pleasure as she came, because I'd witnessed the alluring obedience with which she'd accepted Rafe's fingers in her mouth.

It was not because Rafe was wearing one of those suits that made him look like a magazine ad for unethically expensive watches. It was not because of the easy, graceful power he had as he brought Marian off, as he casually shoved his fingers into her mouth, as he ignored the thick erection pressing against the front of his suit trousers.

It was not because he was handsome and cruel and interesting. It would never be because of that.

At least, never again.

But once they saw me, I'd known I'd miscalculated. Not because of anything I'd predicted about them, but because of what I hadn't predicted about *myself*. About my reaction to seeing the two of them together: one part fury, one part jealousy. Several parts undiluted lust.

"Lox," Rafe said, his eyes like a clear winter sky as he looked at me. He kept his fingers in Marian's mouth. "Welcome."

Marian was so deep in subspace that I don't think anything could have surprised her, but even so, I would've thought my appearance would have had some discernible impact. Something other than that come-drunk stare and post-orgasm panting, at least. Maybe I was becoming predictable—though I doubted it—or maybe she'd secretly hoped I'd come tonight...

Or maybe Rafe was as good as he'd ever been, and Marian was blitzed out of her goddamn mind with the best neurotransmitters and hormones kink had to offer.

But while Rafe seemed like he'd expected me—which confirmed that he'd known I was here in Sherwood—a quick, assessing flick of his eyes from Marian's face to mine told me that he had expected *her* to be more surprised at the sight of me.

Which meant she hadn't told him about my little visit last night.

Good girl.

Rafe slid his fingers free of Marian's plush mouth and wiped them on a handkerchief he pulled from his suit pocket. "To what do we owe the pleasure of your visit tonight, Robin?" he asked. His voice was pleasant, conversational even, but I knew him better than that. I knew he was seething under that veneer of cool control.

"I thought I'd drop in and see how you were topping these days," I said, setting my helmet down on a nearby table with a *thunk*. "Come on, Rafe. Why do you think I'm here?"

Rafe wasn't looking at me as I stepped closer, his eyes on Marian's skin as he ran a careful palm over her punished thighs and bottom. Then he tugged the sheer white fabric of her dress back over her body and scooped her into his arms, already on his way to the low bed in the center of the room.

With the fluttering dress and the garters and the drugged gaze, she looked just like a bride who'd been thoroughly ravished after the ceremony, and Rafe the dashing groom with her in his arms. The jealousy hit me like a wall of fire, but the fire was something else too, something so close to loneliness and lust both that I couldn't pick it apart from everything else.

"I *don't* know why you're here, Lox," Rafe said as he laid Marian down on the bed and covered her with a blanket. She blinked at me from across the room, still floating like a kite in subspace, and my fingers curled in my palms as I watched Rafe tug the ponytail holder from the bottom of her braid and efficiently unravel the plait as he sat down on the edge of the bed.

That should be me. She should be blissed as hell because of *me*, welted and sore because of *me*.

His voice was quieter now, losing a little of that calculated pleasantry. "I can't say it was wise of you to come."

"I suppose that remains to be seen," I said, although he was right and he knew it. It was stupid to show him how much Marian meant to me. Stupid to prove that I was here in Sherwood after all.

And it was beyond stupid to score my already battered heart with the sight of him gently—and with a care and attention he normally reserved for checking weapons and inspecting abseiling equipment—sliding his hands into Marian's hair and massaging her scalp until she sighed.

Those big eyes fluttered closed, and within only a minute or two, she was falling deep into a subspace nap. Rafe didn't stop massaging her scalp though, only pausing after a moment to tuck the blanket more securely around her shoulder.

I begrudgingly had to admit that he was taking good care of her.

"Why, Rafe?" I asked in a low voice, not wanting to wake our sleeping beauty. "Why her?"

"I think you know why," he responded, without taking his eyes from where his fingers still moved in her hair. From where the silky tresses slid around his hands like dark, dark water.

I felt strangely entranced by the sight, like I could watch him play with her hair for the rest of my life.

"I know you're looking for me, if that's what you're implying," I murmured, still watching his hands. "But why drag her into it? Why use her?"

"I had to assume that if you came back to Sherwood, you'd be tempted to make contact with the mysterious sweetheart you'd always refused to talk to me about. And if I could turn her into an asset..."

It was why Rafe was the best in the world at his job. He understood people and their motivations better than any algorithm or data filter ever would. He knew the difference between information and intelligence.

Unfortunately for him, so did I.

"I would never have implicated her by telling her anything of importance," I said, coming closer to the bed. "You must have known that."

"I know that you loved her." He looked up at me. Only Rafe de Lacy could make looking *up* at someone feel dangerous. Predatory. "I know you've never stopped thinking of her, and that kind of love leads to mistakes. Lapses in judgement."

"You would know," I bit out. Still quietly.

"I would know," he agreed. His voice was tinged with bitterness, and I weirdly hated to hear it. I hadn't wanted to hurt him, but he'd made any other outcome impossible when he'd chosen his country over his soul.

"But really, Lox," he said, "why are you here? If you know I'm looking for you, then you must know that Lackland wants you. Badly."

He didn't sound concerned for my future so much as he sounded curious. Like he wanted to know what he might have missed in his own calculations and plans. We used to calculate together, him and me. Partners, him CIA, me NSA, working together in some of the most dangerous places in the world.

And now we were on opposite sides of the chessboard, moving pieces in anticipation of each other, weighing pawns and studying squares.

"Badly enough that arrest isn't on the table anymore," I added with a sharp smile. "Isn't that right, Rafe?"

His pale gaze was unwavering. "So you know then."

"I know." I'd helped build many of the NSA encryptions they now relied on to send information about me back and forth; I'd long ago planted a little electronic ear in Lackland's office. Only Rafe, with his old-fashioned HUMINT ways, evaded my surveillance. "I know that if you get a hold of me, I won't have the luxury of an arrest."

Nor the luxuries of formal charges, or even of a public trial. I was past that point.

"And so I'll ask you again," he said with that invisible chessboard between us, "why show yourself tonight? I could grab you right now and cuff you to that bench until backup arrived. I could have you in the back of a black SUV heading for the airport before Marian even woke up."

I leaned against the bottom poster of the bed. It was made for kink—sturdy and studded with hooks and rings. "You could, but you won't. Because Lackland wants my machines as much as he wants me. And you know that I'll have put contingencies in place regarding them in the case of my capture. And more importantly, contingencies regarding the data they store."

"Very good," Rafe said. His fingers had moved from massaging Marian's scalp to stroking her hair now. Something not for her, but purely for him. I didn't think I was imagining the possessiveness in his touch when he did it.

"So I have to assume that you'd like to persuade me into cooperating."

"An odd tack to take, given how our last conversation went," he conceded.

"It wasn't much of conversation, if you'll recall," I said dryly. "You tried to kill me."

"In fairness, you tried to kill me first."

I shrugged.

It had been a bad night.

"You know I won't cooperate, Rafe."

"And you know I won't stop." With a final smoothing of Marian's hair, he slid off the bed and stood to face me. "This is treason, Lox. The kind of thing you wouldn't have thought twice about stopping only a year ago. The secrets you're stealing..."

"Needed to be stolen. Corruption isn't private property."

Rafe ran a hand through his hair. Too long, it was always a little bit too long, and when he tousled it enough that it fell just so over his forehead, I could almost see the boy he must have been, transplanted by his American mother from his childhood in England, restless and bored and absolutely disdainful of what anyone might call an ordinary life.

"You should have gone public," he said, dropping his hand. "I still can't understand why you didn't. There's a reason Assange and Snowden put themselves in front of every camera they could find, put their names into every paper that would print them. So that if they were caught, they'd be arrested and given a trial, and not...well. *Disappeared.* I know you know this, so there must be something I'm missing."

"Stop trying to reconnoiter me," I said irritably. "I'm not going to explain my motivations to you. I tried hard enough the last time."

We stared at each other, and I remembered, I remembered how vast the gulf had been between us the night I'd fled my assignment, the night I'd tried to convince him that what the NSA was doing was *wrong*. And not wrong in the "some decisions require difficult moral calculus that not everyone will agree with" sense. I'd been a deployed Ranger in the 75th and a covert paramilitary officer over the course of my career—I was no stranger to difficult moral calculus. No, this had been wrong in a whole new way. *Everyone* was being lied to—even the President—about the goals the NSA and CIA were really working toward.

And about whom those agencies were really working for.

And if we defined treason as we ought to define it—as betraying the *people* of a nation, as betraying that nation's best self—then what those agencies were doing was treason full stop.

The problem was that Rafe de Lacy—the half-British boy who'd joined the Army the day after 9/11 and who'd dedicated his entire life to this country—had seen my leaving as the real treason instead.

It hadn't gone well.

And we were at the same impasse today. Except somehow the last person in the world I'd wanted involved was in the middle of it.

"Don't use her, Rafe. I'm asking you. Please."

"And so what should I do? Go back to Lackland and tell him I found you, but leveraging a full recovery of your machines would have involved your ex-girlfriend, and I decided to respect your romantic history instead? At the price of our national security?"

"She's not my ex-girlfriend," I corrected, "and I'm not telling you to do that, because I already know you'd never do it. I'm asking you to find another way. Because she's better than this. She's..."

We both looked down at her, sleeping on the bed like a fairy-tale princess, one pale hand hanging off the edge. Her lips were parted in sleep; I could see a small blotch of blue ink on her ring finger, likely from a rogue fountain pen. I knew from shadowing her emails today that she'd spent her morning in the mycelial research lab and her afternoon finalizing her acquisition of a small firm specializing in algal biofuel. At only twenty-three, she ran her family's green tech corporation with a vision and determination that bordered on apostolic.

Did he know that?

Did he know that this pretty, elegant submissive was already changing the world? Fighting investors, politicians, shareholders, and rivals? And *winning*?

"She's good," Rafe said, so quietly that I barely heard him. I shot my gaze over to his face. He was still looking at her, and the expression he wore then was like nothing I'd ever seen on his face. It was almost awed. Almost tender. "She's good, Lox. I know that. She's not like us."

No, she wasn't like us at all. She worked to make the world better in the broad light of day; she pushed back against greed and destruction not with *more* greed and destruction, but with science and transparency and...grace.

She gave grace to people.

Rafe and I did not give grace to people. Our jobs had never been about grace, only about solving problems. A dark kind of math, done with the darkest kind of science.

Seeing Rafe look at Marian like that made something in my throat ache. "She's not like us," I echoed. "Please."

He didn't answer, his eyes still on the sleeping submissive, his thumb rubbing restlessly at his fingers.

And then Marian's eyes fluttered open. After several bemused blinks, she sat straight up.

"I'm so sorry," she said, her cheeks burning a bright pink. "I—I never do that. Just fall asleep like that."

"It's natural for the end of a scene," Rafe said. When he spoke to her, the roughness in his voice sounded intimate. *Kind*, even, if not totally safe. "How do you feel?"

"Amazing," she said, her eyes sliding over to me. When she added, "Sir," I couldn't tell if it was for his benefit or mine.

"I want to talk to you," I told Marian. "Now."

Rafe stepped forward. "Absolutely not. She needs to go home and sleep."

I glared at him. "You aren't her dominant."

"I am right now, and her recovery is my responsibility."

"I'll talk to you, Lox," Marian said, swinging her legs off the bed. "It's okay, Rafe. I promise I'll go straight home after."

His jaw was tight. "Then I'm staying."

"I fucking dare you to try," I said, crossing my arms.

"I accept the dare," he replied, voice soft and silky.

"Stop!" Marian cried as she got to her feet. "Just stop it! I know that the two of you used to be together, but that's no excuse for"—she gestured between Rafe and me—"whatever this is."

For a moment—an absurd, nearly comical moment—Rafe and I looked at each other and seemed to realize at the same time that she still didn't know the entire truth, or even most of it. *Ex-lovers* was the category she'd filed us under—just normal, run of the mill *ex-lovers*—and maybe that was for the best. *Traitor/hunter of traitors* was a much more complicated category. Especially when the hunter and hunted were also ex-lovers anyway.

And with that look, we agreed.

She didn't need to know any more than she already did at the moment. At least not yet.

"Very well," Rafe said tightly. "I shall leave. But I'll be checking in with you tomorrow, Marian. And as for you, Lox," he said, buttoning his suit jacket and walking toward the door, "I'll be seeing you soon."

His meaning was clear. The chess game wasn't over; he was only hitting the button on his side of the clock. He'd be back.

I wouldn't have expected any less.

Once he left, I turned to face Marian, who was smoothing her hair over her shoulder in preparation for rebraiding it. For a heady moment, I remembered the way she'd been wearing it the afternoon I'd left for deployment, in a ponytail tied with a ribbon which had matched her pretty yellow dress. I'd grabbed hold of that ponytail while I fucked her mouth, and when I'd left, I'd still had that ribbon tangled in my fingers.

It was currently tied around the wooden rail at the head of my bed.

"Well?" Marian asked, deftly separating her hair into three strands.

I walked over and took the strands from her. With a hitch in her breath, she dropped her hands and allowed me.

"I want to keep you safe from Rafe de Lacy," I said as I began weaving her hair into a braid. I went slowly, enjoying the cool weight of it in my hands. "I want to keep you far, far away from him."

"But you know you can't," Marian said, correctly guessing what I was going to say next.

"But I know I can't. So I'm asking you. Marian, please stay away from him."

"You know, it's funny," Marian said, in a voice that told

me she didn't think it was funny at all, "that all I wanted for literal years was for you to come back and take charge of me. For you to make me yours—*no*, for you to realize that I was already yours and all you had to do was claim me."

"Little fox—"

"But now here you are," she went on, "*late*. Here you are after I finally swallowed your rejection, after I finally realized you were never coming back, that you never wanted me to be yours in the first place."

She was so wrong. She couldn't be more wrong than she was at this very moment.

"I've always wanted you," I said fiercely. "Don't you remember the fox game? In the woods?"

Her chin lifted. "Yes," she said. "I remember."

The whole horde of us as children in Sherwood, running wild in the woods together. We'd been animals, all of us, but only Marian and I had been foxes. I was the king fox and she was my queen fox, and Sherwood was our kingdom, the forest was our castle. And even though we eventually outgrew the fox game, I'd never outgrown my queen fox, my consort.

"I knew even then that you were mine. That afternoon, the day I left—I would have it be like that every day if I could." I finished braiding her hair, finding the ponytail holder on the low table near the bed and securing the end of her braid. I wanted to wrap that braid around my hand so badly that I was trembling as I let go of it. "Even now, all I want is to be your king fox again."

"Then why, Lox? Why abandon me, ignore me? Why only come back now?"

I leaned my forehead against hers, letting out a long breath. "I already told you. I'm not safe."

"Good. I don't like safe people anyway."

I had to laugh. The only two people Marian Fitzwalter had ever knelt for were some of the most unsafe people in the world. She knew her own preferences, I'd give her that.

"I don't forgive you for the last five years," she said softly.

"Good. You shouldn't." I didn't forgive myself for them.

"And I'm guessing you have some bullshit reason about why you can't be with me now?"

"Yes," I said, and then I kissed her.

Her mouth was just as soft as I'd remembered, all give and all silk, like the mouth of someone in a dream. Heat licked down into my cunt, reminding me of how it felt to have her kiss on my body, how it felt to have her kneeling in front of me with her ready for my use.

How had I gone five years without feeling her mouth against mine? How had I gone all those years before it?

I lifted my hands to her face and used my thumbs to part her lips so I could slide my tongue against hers. She let me, opened for me. Let me take what I wanted.

Heaven.

She tasted like mint and faintly of expensive gloss, and she panted against my lips as I fucked her with my tongue.

"Don't see him anymore," I murmured between kisses. "Promise me you won't."

"No," she said.

I broke the kiss. She was still breathing hard, and through that sheer nothing of a dress and the thin silk of her bra, I could see the outline of her erect nipples.

"Little fox," I murmured. "What will it take?"

She stepped back, her blue eyes almost purple in the red light of the club. "I want to say that it would take you staying with me—or taking me with you wherever it is you go. Taking me no matter how dangerous you think you are, no matter how much you think I'd be better off without you. But I don't think that's enough anymore." She let out a short, unhappy laugh. "And it's not like you would do it, even if it could be enough."

I wanted to argue with her, but I couldn't. She was right.

I couldn't stay with her, not in the real world where I was wanted for treason, and I wouldn't rip her away from her life and her work to join me as a modern-day outlaw. She deserved better than the trouble either of those options would bring.

"So I guess the answer is that there's nothing you can say to convince me not to see Rafe," she said. She moved over to the door and began putting on her shoes. "At least he's willing to take what I want to give."

"He wants to take so much more than that," I said, torn between telling her the entire truth and keeping her as separate as possible from the mess I'd made. "You can't trust him, Marian. I mean that."

Marian stood and put her hand on the door handle. She looked back at me. "But why should I trust you instead?" she asked. And she didn't wait for an answer.

She left.

CHAPTER

SIX

RAFE

ONE WEEK LATER

A far blue sky stretched overhead, echoed by the expanse of ocean below. Gulls and cormorants wheeled through the air, and the water rolled endlessly forward, foaming and sizzling as it died away on the khaki-colored sand of the beach.

Marian sat on a blanket on the sand, her feet bare and her hair ruffling in the summer breeze. The beach was small, narrow, girded by rocky cliffs on either side and sheltered by tree-capped sea stacks, and even the trees on actual, proper land still felt like sentinels around us. It felt more defensible than actual outposts I'd built and manned. It felt like a castle made of sea and sky.

"Thank you for meeting me," I said as I reached her.

Marian looked up from where she sat on the blanket, a small smile creasing those full lips. "Is that your idea of a beach outfit?"

I looked down at my suit trousers and brogues. "I came from a meeting," I said as I sat down next to her. That much was true.

"Here in Sherwood?" she asked curiously.

"In Olympia," I replied, also honestly, as I pulled off my brogues and dress socks, and then rolled up the cuffs of my suit pants. "Better?"

The smile was much bigger now. "That's not good for your suit, you know."

"Clothes were made to be worn, Marian. And I see why you suggested we meet here. It's lovely."

"It is," Marian said. She pulled her knees up to her chest and rested her head on them. Her eyes settled on the birds, on the sea stacks beyond. "I like coming here after I've been in the city. It reminds me of who I am. Really am, I mean."

A specific kind of satisfaction rolled through me as she spoke, as it became clear that she was beginning to trust me. I would wonder if it was the satisfaction of the dominant or the spy, but I gave up trying to splice my various selves apart long ago. What made me good at one made me good at the other, and I wasn't bothered by that.

What I was bothered by was that I found this new trust of hers unhealthily tempting. I didn't want to leverage it so much as I wanted to eat it. I wanted her to trust me with everything—her thoughts, her flesh, her *breath*—and I wanted everything to start right now, here on the cool, damp sand of the beach.

Or perhaps I'd wanted it to start before, from the moment I'd felt her come around my fingers, from the moment I witnessed her adorable indignation as I betrayed her with the silicone paddle.

This whole arrangement was supposed to be about Lox,

and it *was* about Lox, but there was only so far I could justify my fascination with Marian as being related to the mission. And there was certainly only so far I could explain away the visceral impatience I'd felt to see her again. I'd cultivated assets over weeks and months—over years, even—and yet this week while she'd been working at her office in Seattle had nearly driven me mad.

"I missed you," I said without meaning to, but it was the right thing to say, because she flushed and swallowed. And then gave me a look that bordered on happy.

"I missed you too," she said, a little shyly.

"How was your week in the city?" I asked. "Busy?"

She didn't move, but I could see the renewed tension in her arms and shoulders. "Yes," she answered after a moment. "Very busy." She looked like she wanted to say more but was forcing herself not to. My guess was that she wanted to tell me, but telling me would reveal more about her life and her job than she was ready for me to know.

I studied her and came to a decision. "When we started this, I asked you to answer my questions honestly. I think it's only fair that I return the courtesy, or at least the spirit of the courtesy, and be honest with you."

Blue eyes flicked to mine, confused.

"I know your last name," I said gently. "I know where you work and why you work there."

She turned her face away, into her knees.

It was such dominant-bait, that skittish, submissive pose, and need rolled down my stomach and thighs as I watched her. I wanted to uncurl her and flatten her against the sand. Wedge myself between her thighs and bite at her throat and jaw and mouth until she understood that she wasn't allowed to hide from me. Not ever.

"You said it was okay if I didn't give you my name at all," she mumbled. "If I only gave you a pseudonym."

"I'm not accusing you of lying, sweet one. I'm just telling you what I know. I'm telling you that you don't have to pretend you're not helming a ship worth hundreds of millions of dollars."

"How did you find out?" she asked, still talking into her knees.

This. This would be a lie. A necessary one, but I found I regretted it all the same. "Your profile in *Forbes* this week. Very impressive."

She turned the tiniest amount, to where I could see the pert curve of her nose. She let out a resigned sigh. "The bartender at The Knot told me that you were here for an ecological survey. I didn't want you to think..."

"That you were sleeping with me so Fitzwalter Green would have a friend inside the EPA?" I suggested.

She made a noise. Almost a laugh. "Yes. Ridiculous, I know."

"Marian, I can promise you that I matter very, very little to the EPA," I said, which was the truth. "So set your mind at ease. Even if our arrangement becomes public knowledge, you won't be accused of lobbying or corruption."

She finally turned her head to look at me. "I'm relieved you know who I am," she admitted. "This last week has been busy. Hard. I kept thinking it would feel easier if I had someone to spank the stress out of me every night."

My cock pulsed at the thought. I reached for her wrist and pulled, carefully. Testing. When she didn't resist, I moved in front of her, resting on my knees, and took her other wrist in my hand. I pulled her hands to the blanket and then kept them there with my own. She stared at me.

"You can say *red* or *yellow*," I reminded her.

She sank her teeth into her lower lip and then slowly shook her head. "It feels good," she admitted. "Being held down."

"Of course it does. I'll ask you a question, and then you answer me. Why was this week hard?"

There was more resistance to answering this than to being pinned by her hands to the blanket, but I saw her surrender all the same. It sped my pulse, but I kept myself still for her, ready to receive this little sacrifice of hers.

For the mission, I thought distantly. *Only for the mission.*

Yeah, right.

"When I decided to take on the business, I wanted to honor my parents. Do you know what my family is? What they used to be?"

I did, and had known from the thick, well-thumbed folder on Marian I currently had next to my bed at the safehouse, but luckily for this moment, it had also been in the *Forbes* profile. "Lumber barons."

"There's no telling how much damage they did to the forests in those days," she said. "They took without thinking, and even by the flawed definition of land ownership in this country, they took from land that didn't belong to them. That's the legacy my father was born into, the legacy he hated. He's the one who converted the old mills and switched to sustainable lumber. He's the one who founded Fitzwalter Green and invested in green technology and infrastructure. He wanted to heal what our family had done. He wanted to atone."

"And so do you."

Marian closed her eyes a moment. "It sounds so simple, doesn't it? Atoning. Doing right."

I thought of Lox. I thought of myself. "No," I said. "It doesn't."

She opened her eyes to meet mine. "It doesn't?"

"Building something that's right—or eliminating something that's wrong—can never be simple. There are compromises, nuances. Realities that can't be shifted no matter what your ideals are."

She breathed out. "So you understand."

"Why wouldn't I?"

"Lox wouldn't," she said quietly. "Lox despised the kinds of compromises and nuances we're talking about now. Which I suppose you already know."

Yes, I did. "So this week. Your company is trying to bring new ideas into a world that doesn't understand them and sometimes doesn't want them at all, and day after day, you feel like you're losing something invaluable, a purity of vision, a virginity of cause."

"Yes," she said, looking down at the sand. "We need money to do good in this world. But sometimes I worry I'm doing less than the good I could be doing in order to make that money. And around the cycle goes, until I feel lost inside myself, until I feel like I don't even know who I really am or what I really believe."

I held her hands down a little tighter. Tight enough that she shivered, and then she let out a long, shaky breath.

"Thank you," she whispered.

"Always," I said, and when I said it, I realized I meant it.

Which was not a good thing.

"Lox would never have this problem," Marian murmured. "She knows herself and she'd never do something to betray her own mind."

"But Lox would betray other people," I said, my voice

sounding harsh even to my own ears, and I let out a sharp breath, wishing I hadn't spoken.

Marian studied me. Not warily, but carefully. "And are you one of them?" she asked. "One of the betrayed?"

I could almost laugh at how ridiculous this was. Here I was pinning an asset to the ground, and she was questioning me on the very subject I'd engaged her for. But as I looked into her deep blue eyes, I found I couldn't untangle myself from this topsy-turvy moment. Not yet.

"Yes," I said, quietly.

"I'm sorry to hear that," she said, also quietly.

For a moment, there was only the push and hiss of the waves as they fussed their way onto the shore. Only the birds overhead and the sun glowing down to spite the rain that had fallen earlier this morning.

Marian's stare was as endless as the ocean behind me, and even as I held her down, I felt myself drowning in it.

Lox, was this how you felt? Bold and fierce as you were, you still couldn't stop drowning in Marian's eyes?

"Why did you want to meet me?" Marian finally whispered, and I had to regain control, I had to remember why I was here. There would be so much truth in what I told her next and still so many lies—and the next time we played together would be much the same.

If I didn't move the pieces just right, Lox would take the board. Checkmate.

I let go of Marian's hands, but before the instinctive frown of disappointment could settle on her lips, I was already pushing her down and crawling over her. I used my hips to pin hers, my thighs trapping hers neatly between them, and I kept myself braced on my elbows.

"This is nice," she breathed.

It was nice. So nice that I was already painfully, achingly hard.

But this wasn't for me. This was for what came next.

"I wanted to see you because I like you, Marian. I want to see more of you, and I want us to play. I want us to play as much as we can. But after the way we left things, I know you might have questions for me. Things you'd like to ask or say that are harder to speak aloud in a kink club."

Marian let out a long breath. "You think Lox tried to talk me out of seeing you after you left."

"Didn't she?"

"Yes."

I wasn't bothered by that. I'd almost be disappointed if she hadn't.

"I have no right to ask you what she said or implied about me, so I'm not going to. But I want you to know that you can ask me anything you'd like about myself or about my relationship with her. I don't want our past with Lox to interrupt what we have now."

"And what do we have now?" Marian murmured, her eyes searching mine.

How could it have been so, so true for me to say what I said next? "Whatever you want," I told her.

More birds. More waves. I knew the way Marian was assessing me because I did it to her, because I did it as my job.

I also knew what she would see as she looked at me: a dominant who was quickly growing obsessed with her. It was what I wanted her to see; it had always been the plan for her to see it.

It just so also happened to be the truth.

"How did you meet Lox?" Marian finally asked. "And when?"

"Two years ago," I said. "I was doing a footprint survey for an expansion of the NSA campus at Fort Meade, getting into stupid fights about the size of parking lots and the location of solar panels. I found an unexpected ally in her. She'd been a Ranger, I'd been a Green Beret. We immediately recognized something in each other, I suppose."

Except for the Ranger and Green Beret part, this was entirely a lie. I met Robin Loxley for the first time on a freezing, muddy mission in Carpathia, and we'd starting fighting the moment we met. We never stopped, really, not even after we fell into bed and I fell into reckless, miserable love.

"Unfortunately," I finished now, "we were far too much alike to make it last."

"Because you're both dominants."

Laying on her like this, braced on my elbows, left my hands free to play with her hair as I spoke. "Lox and I were mismatched from the start, and I knew it. But I believed it wouldn't matter. What was dominance but the way we liked to fuck? Surely that wouldn't affect anything else, *couldn't* affect anything else?"

Marian didn't say anything, and I gave a small, unhappy smile at her silence. "I see you can guess that it did affect things, in the end. There were other factors in our split, but that was the root of it. Neither of us could bend, so we broke instead."

Marian bit her lip. "Why does she think you'll hurt me?"

Because she knows I'm using you. Because she knows that I'll choose my job—my country—over someone I love with my whole heart.

"She used to call me a wolf, and it's not...an inaccurate word. I am greedy, Marian, I am ravenous. I won't hesitate to devour you if you let me."

She trembled a little underneath me, and I felt the unconscious lift of her hips against mine at my words. She liked that.

I liked it too.

"Can you tell that I'm jealous?" Marian asked, a twist to her mouth. "That the two of you were together?"

"Marian, I've been jealous of you for two years."

Her lips parted. "You have?"

I could have laughed if it didn't still sting so much.

"You know Lox—emphatic and transparent to the last. She told me everything I ever wanted to know about her, except when it came to you. You were the only secret she kept, the only answer she wouldn't give. Once, when drunk, she confessed to me that the memory of you followed her around like a ghost. Another time, she told me that if she ever died, her last breath would be speaking your name. I loved her, and she loved a girl she'd left behind and couldn't bring herself to see again. You can see how I'd have occasion for jealousy, I think."

"But..."

I couldn't believe I was saying what I said next, from a professional or a self-preservation standpoint, but the dominant in me needed to give her this. "Whatever reasons she's had for staying away, or even for leaving in the first place, it wasn't because she didn't love you, Marian. If you know nothing else, please know that."

Marian closed her eyes a moment.

"I don't know what to think," she said, her voice tight. "It feels impossible to trust that she could care for me that much and yet still stay away..."

"Maybe Lox knows more about difficult compromises than we give her credit for."

Marian opened her eyes. "And you? Are you still in love with her?"

I didn't want to answer that question. I didn't want to answer it at all.

But I did.

"Yes," I said, the word scraping its way like gravel up my throat. I was surprised I didn't taste blood after I spoke it. "Yes, I'm still in love with her."

Seeing Lox at the club last week had been like a punch to the chest followed by a fist around my cock. I hadn't needed to see her bright eyes or hear her husky voice to know that I still loved her, but her appearance at the club made the truth impossible to ignore.

In love with my mark and obsessed with my asset. Not good.

"Then I'm sorry," Marian said, sounding sincere, and I sighed.

"Me too."

"We're really fucked up, aren't we?"

I looked down at her and traced the edge of her jaw with a finger. "In my life, most things are fucked up. That doesn't mean they're not good."

She turned her head enough to nip at my fingertip. Pleasure seared up the nerves of my arm.

Yes, this was getting more and more dangerous by the moment.

"Rafe," she said, kissing my finger before turning back to me. "Will you keep doing this? Telling me the truth too?"

"Yes," I said. "I'll tell you the truth always."

It was a lie. And as long as I had this job, it would always be a lie. Maybe that was one of the reasons I'd fallen so swiftly in love with Lox. With a mission partner, there didn't have to be secrets, lies, half-truths.

How briefly wonderful that had been.

"Final question," Marian asked. "Can we play again soon?"

My cock jumped against her, both from the promise of having her again and from the cold little victory I'd just achieved.

"Yes, darling. I even had an idea about that today. What would you say to making one of the things on your wish list come true?"

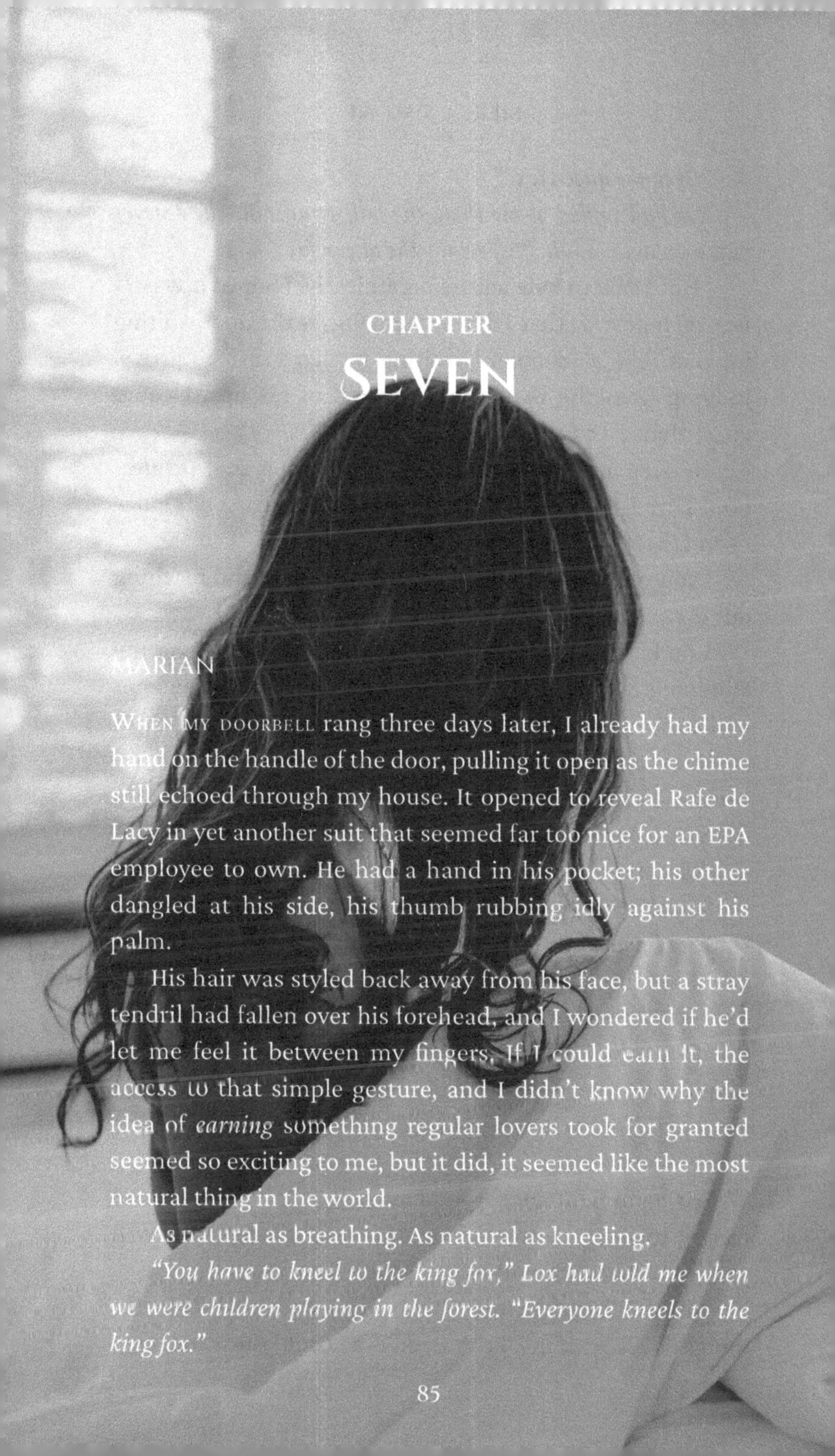

CHAPTER

SEVEN

MARIAN

WHEN MY DOORBELL rang three days later, I already had my hand on the handle of the door, pulling it open as the chime still echoed through my house. It opened to reveal Rafe de Lacy in yet another suit that seemed far too nice for an EPA employee to own. He had a hand in his pocket; his other dangled at his side, his thumb rubbing idly against his palm.

His hair was styled back away from his face, but a stray tendril had fallen over his forehead, and I wondered if he'd let me feel it between my fingers. If I could earn it, the access to that simple gesture, and I didn't know why the idea of *earning* something regular lovers took for granted seemed so exciting to me, but it did, it seemed like the most natural thing in the world.

As natural as breathing. As natural as kneeling.

"You have to kneel to the king fox," Lox had told me when *we were children playing in the forest. "Everyone kneels to the king fox."*

"Even the queen fox?"

Lox had smiled at me then, the half-feral smile she'd never lost, even as an adult. "Especially the queen fox."

"Hi," I said to Rafe a little breathlessly. I hoped it wasn't *incredibly obvious* that I'd been hanging by the door waiting for him, like a schoolgirl waiting for her crush to arrive. Judging from the barely-there twitch of his lips, I could guess that it was more obvious than I'd like.

He stepped into my house—only giving the *Architectural Digest*-featured surroundings a quick, cursory glance—and then he settled his cool gaze on me.

"You waited to get dressed," he said, his hand reaching out to run along the flat lapel of my robe. "Good."

I nodded as his fingers drifted lower, ghosting over my stiffening nipples under the silk and then finding the knot of the robe's belt and hooking his fingers behind it. With an embarrassingly small motion, he was able to yank me close—close enough that I could see the individual eyelashes framing his pale winter-sky eyes.

"Is it still okay?" he asked. "If I dress you tonight?"

Yes, and please dress me every night for the rest of time.

"Yes," I murmured as I blinked up at him. This close, I could see that his mouth was softer than it looked at first. The sharp geometry of it belied the subtle curves of his lips, the oh-so-slight tilts at the very edges, as if God had given him a mouth for boyish smiles and dangerous smirks and Rafe had simply chosen to brood with it instead. "I like the idea of you dressing me."

His hand tightened around my belt before he let go and turned to shut the front door. "Me too," he replied. "Will you show me what clothes you have?"

On the beach when he'd suggested the idea for tonight's scene to me, he'd asked if he could dress me for it too. "It's okay if the answer is no," he'd said. He'd still been braced over me then, his thighs and arms caging me deliciously on the sand, and his erection pressing hard into my stomach. "Helping you dress will be blurring the lines between us, bringing our interactions outside the structure of a scene."

"And this isn't?" I'd asked, and he'd searched my face.

"You're right. I'm already blurring the lines with you."

"Blur them. Sir."

And so now here we were, blurring all sorts of lines as he walked through my house to my bedroom and into my walk-in closet, ready to thumb through my clothes to see what I should be wearing when I was tied and spread for anyone who happened to be at the club tonight.

Rafe looked through my closet with a brisk but hungry efficiency that made me wet to watch. He'd flip past several things only to stop at one and bring it to his nose. His fingers would trail over the fabric and then he'd find its hem, testing how much access the dress would give him, before returning it to its place and moving on to the next. Finally, he stopped at a red one—a filmy, sleeveless number with a deep V neckline and a high slit up the side.

"This one," he said with complete certainty.

"Are you sure you wouldn't rather I wear something...I don't know...kinkier?"

He pulled the hanger from the rod and rehung it on a hook fastened to the closet door. "Do you think you should show up to the club wearing PVC and a harness?"

I laughed. "I mean, a little. This dress is very colorful."

"It's very Marian Fitzwalter, and Marian Fitzwalter gets me hard. Come here."

I approached him, and again he hauled me close by the knot of my belt, his eyes bent to his work as he untied the fabric and made short work of my robe. When he saw the lacy black bra and panties I wore underneath, his eyes darkened.

"If I had my way, I would take these pretty underthings off with my teeth. But alas, we are limited on time this evening. May I take these off the ordinary way instead?"

I had no objection to him undressing me, but the idea of showing up to the club without panties felt scandalous somehow. Which was silly, since the whole point was to expose myself to everyone anyway, but still.

Correctly interpreting my look, Rafe said, "I want your cunt available right away. And Marian, as much as I enjoy all these expensive knickers of yours, I want you naked under your clothes whenever we meet, unless you've come from work or unless I specify otherwise. Understood?"

Oh, I understood. And when he framed it like that, I never wanted to wear underwear again.

"Consider them gone, sir," I said, and he smiled. Without another word, he tugged the panties off my hips and down to my ankles, where he carefully guided my feet out of the lace. Then he unhooked my bra and exposed my breasts to the cool air of the room.

When he finished, he folded the lingerie into a neat pile and set it on my bed. Though his demeanor remained cool and reserved, I heard his inhale as he looked at my naked body in its entirety. But his control remained intact, and he turned to take the dress off its hanger.

"Tell me about the past few days," he said. "I want to know how you've been feeling."

I groaned. "Part of the allure of kink for me is that I want you to tell me how to feel."

A low laugh. "I suppose that's its own answer. Arms up."

I obeyed, and he settled the dress over me without disturbing my hair, which I'd already styled.

"It's been the same since we talked last," I finally answered. He guided the dress down around my hips and then smoothed the skirt. His touch was a strange combination of preemptory and comforting. "We're acquiring a biofuel company, mostly for their algal products and ongoing R&D. However, they've been earning the money to fund their algal research by producing ethanol made from corn too, which is environmentally problematic. But objectively lucrative. Some in my company want to divest from the ethanol products immediately, and some think we should keep them, because *someone* is going to make ethanol, and at least if it's us, we can use that money to do good things."

Rafe swept the hair off my neck and draped it carefully over my shoulder. "And what do you think? And remember you are to be honest with me. I'm not interested in what you believe you *should* think."

I stared out the large window that made up the far wall of my bedroom. It looked out over the same view as the windows in the living room and kitchen, nothing but rocks and sea and sinking orange sun.

I was grateful that he'd commanded my honesty, because I found the answer much faster than I normally would have. "I think they're both missing something crucial, which is that those ethanol products represent a huge source of income for a substantial number of farmers. I agree we should stop selling it, but find a way to stop that doesn't leave the farmers who count on us to buy their corn in the lurch. And I think it's okay if it takes us a few months to find the smartest way to do it."

It wouldn't be how Lox would do it, probably. If she felt

like something was the right thing to do, she did it immediately. Joining the Army had been like that, even though she'd only just finished studying mathematics at MIT. And I assumed however she'd gone on the run had been much the same too.

She decided quickly, then she acted even quicker.

I wasn't sure if I'd ever be like that, but I wanted to be. Or at the very least, I wanted to be faster at making the kinds of choices I did.

Rafe's fingers brushed against my back as he zipped up the dress. "Don't be ashamed of taking your time. Complicated decisions always benefit from more intelligence."

Intelligence. A strange way to put it.

He seemed to sense that too, because he corrected himself, "Information. Complicated decisions always benefit from more information."

"I worry that gathering more information ends up being an excuse for passivity. I want—I want to find a way to listen to my instinct and rationality both. Just once, I'd like to make a choice because it feels right and not because I've spent months and months thinking it through."

Rafe finished zipping up the dress and his hands smoothed the fabric over my back. His hands were so large and warm, his touch was so arrogant and sure of itself. I loved it. "You are twenty-three and running a corporation that represents your father's legacy and also your hopes and dreams for the world. You are creating space for ideas and products that do not yet exist. I think you can afford yourself some grace. And," he added, his big hands turning my hips to face him, "I think you've already made a choice like that."

Abruptly confronted with that sharp-yet-soft mouth

and that heavy-lidded stare, I found my thoughts scattering like sandpipers before a wave. "I have?" I asked, clueless.

"Yes," he said. His hands moved up to my waist. "You chose me."

I did. I did choose him.

And God help me, it might have been the smartest choice I'd ever made.

My hands found his chest and then slid up to his neck. "Then I must be better at choosing than I give myself credit for, sir."

He pushed me back a step, then two, and then I was pinned between him and the wall, with his hips hard against mine and his hands finding my wrists. He pushed them above my head and held them there as he leaned in and bit my neck.

I cried out, my hips seeking friction, my entire body trying to arch, and then he slanted his mouth over mine for a hot, searching kiss. He parted my lips immediately and plundered, taking like my mouth belonged to him, like all of me belonged to him.

I suddenly wanted that so much that it hurt. To belong. To belong to him. Even though this was temporary, and I would saw my own arm off before I let someone have the power to hurt me like Lox had hurt me.

Rafe broke the kiss to turn me around and shove me against the wall once more, his teeth on my neck and his hands roaming everywhere, rucking up my dress to slide up my thighs and hips.

One large hand cupped my bare pussy, and we both exhaled as it became apparent how wet I was.

"We don't have time to do this the way I want," Rafe said. He sounded calm and collected, and also vaguely remorseful, although the hard press of his hand and the thick rod shoved against my bottom let me know that his remorse was anything but vague. "Later."

"Tonight?" I asked hopefully.

He stepped back, and when I turned, he was adjusting his erection in his suit trousers. "Perhaps," he said. "If you've earned it."

Oh. Earning. I liked that. I liked it enough that I didn't try to persuade him to fuck me now, here and without any delay, even though I was sorely tempted. The bites on my neck were like sparks, kindling flames deep in my cunt.

"Now," Rafe said, as if I'd been the one to interrupt the business of getting dressed by tempting him to kiss me. "Shoes."

He went into the closet, and after a few moments, returned with a pair of red Louboutins. I sat on the edge of my bed and reached for the shoes he was holding.

HE GAVE me a look that made me think of benches and paddles, of the way his fingers felt in my mouth. "Allow me," he said, already coming to a crouch at my feet.

I never would have thought a squat could be graceful, but for Rafe it was. He crouched like a cat—all effortless balance and coiled power—and his suit strained over the hard muscles of his thighs and stretched tight over his back, revealing a body that was made for war, not ecological surveys.

With deft hands, he slid the first high heel onto my foot, and then the second, taking care each time to make sure my toes were fitted properly in the toe box and that my heel was pressed all the way to the sole.

Even crouched, he was at eye level with me, and he

looked at me when he was finished. "Are you ready for tonight?" he asked.

"Yes, sir," I said.

"Are you nervous?"

"Also yes." I wasn't entirely sure why—when I was in college and desperately trying to forget Lox, I'd had enough sex with all sorts of people that it was hard to imagine what I could possibly be nervous about now. In the spirit of honesty, I added, "And a little embarrassed."

"There's no need to be. It's a common fantasy, wanting to be shared." He stood easily and then took my hands to help me to my feet.

"Is it a fantasy of yours too? I mean, from the dominant side?"

A slow breath. "Yes," he said after a minute. "Intensely so."

"Oh," I said.

"To be able to share someone would mean that they're mine to share. I've never had someone be *mine* before, even for the space of a few weeks."

I stared up into that hooded gaze. "Am I yours then, sir?"

He answered quietly, "I want you to be."

My heart thumped hard against my chest and my cheeks burned—with lust or shyness or a flushing happiness, I wasn't sure.

"I want to be," I said. "Even if it's only until your work in Sherwood is done."

A kind of restlessness moved through him then, and I thought I saw a shadow move over his face as he stepped back.

"We should go," he said instead of responding. He was already turning toward the door. "Otherwise we'll be late."

———————

AN HOUR LATER, and I was on a stage in the central room of The Knot.

CUFFED TO A PADDED LEATHER PLATFORM. Blindfolded.

I could hear the steady drumbeats and silky voice of FADE's latest single in the background; the steady tap of Rafe's dress shoes on the floor.

"THANK YOU ALL FOR COMING TONIGHT," Rafe said. His voice wasn't loud, but the room hushed itself nonetheless. The quiet authority in the way he spoke was palpable, arresting. I imagined even other dominants would pause to hear it.

Had Lox paused to hear it, once upon a time? Had she heard another king fox in the forest and decided he was worthy of her claws and her teeth?

"I've been told that it's not uncommon here to have a scene on stage or even to have a submissive up here, available for play, but I wanted to try something new tonight," Rafe told the crowd. "A little game."

There was a renewed murmur at this, and even though I'd already known this was the plan, I still shivered to hear the cold hedonism in his voice. Yes, I wanted this, but I also wanted *not* to want this, I also wanted to be scared of it, scared of him, scared of myself and the hollow bruises inside that begged to be burned away.

I wanted one part of my life—just *one*, please God—to be as immutable as the ocean, as jaggedly bright as lightning. I wanted something that was outside of my control, outside of my responsibility to change or make better, beyond what I could affect or change. I wanted the absence of choice, or at least the pretense of it, and I wanted to feel, however briefly, the totality of someone's will pressed against my own.

And perhaps it was because I'd lost my parents too young or perhaps it was because Fitzwalter Green Technology would never tell me *good girl* in exchange for its whips and welts, but I couldn't help but think I'd been formed like this from the beginning. From the time I was a little girl and another girl told me that the rule was to kneel, and that rule made more sense to me than any other rule I'd ever learned.

"The game is this: whoever makes my submissive come the hardest tonight wins. You can use your fingers, mouths, or any of the toys I've brought up here to do so, and I shall be the one to determine a winner."

"What do we get if we win?" someone asked.

Rafe's hand dropped to my thigh, and I tried to arch toward the touch. The cuffs around my wrists and ankles made it nearly impossible to move at all, but I still twisted. Rafe gave my thigh a sharp slap, the message clear. *Settle down.*

"You might only get bragging rights," he said. "Or you might get more, depending on my mood."

"I like the sound of more," a woman said, and several others agreed.

I liked the sound of more too, but before I could say something to this effect, there was a small cheer and what sounded like another pair of men's dress shoes tapping across the stage to me. Rafe's hand tightened briefly on my thigh—out of reassurance or out of reluctance to surrender me to another person's touch, I wasn't sure—and then he let go. My thigh burned where his touch had been, and I found myself straining for the sound of his footsteps, for the cool murmur of his voice.

I could tell right away that the hand now stroking my arm wasn't Rafe's. It wasn't warm enough, not nearly rough enough. And the careful way it traveled to my shoulder and then back down to my wrist—that wouldn't be Rafe's style at all.

But it still left goosebumps in its wake, it still made me suck in deeper and deeper breaths, because it was a *stranger*, because I was *blindfolded*. Cuffed and spread, the slit of my dress wide open, open enough that I knew my bare cunt would be visible at the right angle.

I could feel the cool air of the room on my sex, and it drove me wild.

The stranger made an approving noise as he sanded his palms over my breasts and my already aching nipples stiffened even more; he wasted no time in weighing me with his hands and thumbing the tips before moving down to my hips and then my thighs.

He paused before pushing his hands under my skirt. "May I?" he asked Rafe, as if I were irrelevant, as if my permission didn't matter. And it didn't. Right now, I was Rafe's—Rafe's to play with, Rafe's to share. Rafe's to hoard if he so chose.

"By all means," Rafe replied, sounding as indifferent as a host being asked if it would be okay to toss a coat on a bed.

The stranger took his time, his touch trembling the slightest bit as he caressed his way up my inner thighs to my cunt. But we both trembled when he found the swollen bud of my clit, which felt as ripe and ready as a summer berry.

I heard movement from the crowd as Rafe's hands

found the silk of my skirt and shoved it up to my waist, impatiently, again like a host having his hospitality ignored. The stranger murmured something to Rafe that I couldn't hear, and then gently rubbed my clit again, sliding his fingers inside of me at the same time. I was so wet that I could hear him do it, I could hear his slow strokes in and out of my vagina, and I knew that people would see it too. See the glisten of how much I liked this.

I could hear the whispers and shifts and sighs, like people were touching themselves to the sight of me being touched, and knowing that, knowing that my eager acquiescence to being handled like a whore was driving people to touch and rub and squeeze, was almost unbearable. Even though the stranger's hands on me were only slightly better than competent, even though so much of me still keened for more, a swift orgasm overtook me, quick and easy. I cried out, softly: Rafe's name.

His now-familiar hand settled once, briefly, over my throat, where a collar would be if I had one, and then disappeared.

There was clapping, Rafe congratulating the stranger. And then the click of high heels, the feel of narrow, long-nailed hands, and it began all over again.

This contestant used a vibrator, which brought me off quickly and efficiently. Another person used a thumb on my clit and a hot mouth on my breasts. Another went down on me from the start, eating me as fastidiously as a cat licking cream, but it still got the job done. I came with Rafe's name on my lips for a fourth time, and then slumped back onto the platform.

"I like that you keep saying my name, darling," Rafe said. I didn't think I was imagining the cool pleasure in his voice, since his hands had been on me more and more as the night went on, as if he couldn't stop himself from touching me. From sticking his fingers in my mouth or tracing the arch of my throat or pressing his hand against my heart to feel it beat against my ribs. "It makes me think you know all your orgasms belong to me right now."

"They do, sir," I mumbled. I felt wild, dazed, wrung out. Turned out that there could be too much of a good thing: four orgasms was *plenty* for this CEO. "I don't think I can take any more."

"Hmm," said Rafe. That didn't sound like it boded well for me.

"Please," I whimpered, too tired to properly beg. "I don't think I can do any more."

"Is this a red? Or a yellow?"

I stopped. Swallowed. Tried to think. It wasn't a *red*, I knew that for sure, but a *yellow*...? My pussy felt swollen and hot, and my nipples and clit ached from being sucked on so much. I knew I'd be sore tomorrow as it was, and anything more would turn that soreness into *ouch*.

But then Rafe's hand found my throat again, stroking and tracing, and I forgot exactly what it was I was asking for. I forgot everything that wasn't him, that wasn't what he wanted, and I slowly shook my head.

"Still green, sir."

A quick squeeze around my throat, and then I felt his hands on either side of my head as he bent down to whisper in my ear. "One more, sweet one. Give me one more." His words were warm, growled gently in that faint British accent, and I couldn't deny them even if I'd wanted to. And who would want to?

"Yes, sir," I said, and he nipped at my jaw in response, like a wolf pleased with its mate.

And then I heard the first gasp.

It was almost comically loud, that noise, loud enough to carry over the heavy music and the blood still rushing through my ears from the last orgasm. But then I heard the second gasp and an ensuing wave of murmurs, which crested like a wave as I felt Rafe pull away from me.

Boots thudded across the stage, measured and heavy, and then they stopped.

There were no words between this new stranger and Rafe, but I sensed that there was still some kind of exchange. Of looks or gestures, I didn't know, but the tension between them was an electric thing, a current of humming, buzzing hostility.

Fingertips, cool and dry, ran from my chin to the flat expanse of my sternum. The other contestants had gone carefully, almost hesitatingly, but not this one. After splaying a hand over my chest, as if to make a lid over my heart, the stranger pushed their other hand up my skirt and curled their hand over my pussy, sending renewed fire licking and flickering everywhere.

And then: the scent of cedar and loam, sweet and rich.

The smell of Sherwood itself.

Hope—that dizzy, half-melancholy bitch—leapt nervously in my chest. It couldn't be her—it would be pathetic to wish for it to be her—especially since she hadn't tried to find me or talk to me since that night in the castle room.

She'd given up on me, of that I was certain, or had at the very least shoved me to the back of her mind.

But there was something about this new contestant's touch...something so arrogant and practically autocratic in its categorical certainty that my body was theirs to toy with. That my body was there for them, their pleasure, their amusement, and I would submit to their handling without complaint or delay. The arrogance I would have responded to from anyone, I was sure, but that *certainty*...

Only Rafe and one other person had ever touched me like that.

The stranger found my breasts, and—still holding onto my cunt with a strength that was nearly cruel—began teasing the already well-loved peaks, pinching and rolling my nipples until heat had strung a taut web between my chest and my clit and I was twisting in my bonds, arching for more. I hadn't thought I could come again, I hadn't thought I could even *handle* the possibility of coming again, and yet within a moment, I was already panting for it, straining for it.

"Please," I begged. "Please, *please*."

The stranger didn't respond and Rafe stayed silent, but I heard the crowd responding to my response, stirring, sighing. Moaning. Just beyond my blindfold, there was a sea of people kissing and stroking and so much more.

Just beyond my blindfold, there was Rafe de Lacy, watching me with those hooded eyes, and just beyond my blindfold, there was a stranger bunching my dress in their hands to drag it all the way up to my chest so that everything below my ribs was exposed. My navel, my hips, my sex.

All of it was available to them and to the audience, and would it be so twisted if I allowed myself to believe it was Lox? Would it be so wrong? To imagine that vicious hand between my legs was hers, to decide that it was her breath ghosting over my breast before it was given a hard, lingering bite?

My cries echoed up to the high ceiling of the club, mixing with the thudding music and the crowd's moans, and then that biting mouth moved to my other breast, biting me over the silk of my dress before sucking hard at a nipple. This stranger didn't bother to pull the bodice down or to the side as the others had—the stranger simply sucked and bit through the fabric, greedy and indifferent all at once. And then they moved down again, biting my stomach, licking the rim of my navel, biting the top of one thigh hard enough that a guttural, animal noise tore out of my chest.

The pain was localized and yet it was everywhere too, the bites like burning stars in a constellation I'd waited my entire life to name, and it was as I was panting and keening my way through the searing sensation of it that the stranger slid three fingers inside my pussy.

I was already open from earlier, wet enough for it be humiliating, but the abrupt invasion still had my head thrashing on the platform, my mouth open in a soundless O. The fingers filled and pressed—there was no jabbing or sawing in and out—and as they hooked towards the front of my vagina, the stranger's mouth found my clit and sucked.

There was no fastidiousness here, no hesitation. The stranger sucked hard, licked messily, nipped until I was wild in my restraints, not sure if I was trying to get farther away from or closer to the stranger's brutal, delicious mouth.

And then I felt Rafe's hands on my waist, securing me to the table and holding me as securely as a leather band around my middle. He held me still as the stranger fucked my cunt with a sweet viciousness that made my body sing and my heart soar, and I couldn't hear anything at all anymore, not the noises of the crowd nor the thumping beat of the music, because there was only the blood rushing in my ears and my own desperate, slutty noises—panting breaths, begging moans, and the slick sounds of my spread cunt.

The orgasm, when it came, nearly ripped me apart. It was the blindfold, yes, and the cuffs, and the avaricious gazes of the crowd. It was the strangers that had come before and the orgasms they'd given me. But mostly it was this: Rafe's hands holding me down, the stranger's merciless possession of my body.

Both of them had absolute sovereignty over me in this moment, and the world was magical, electrical, glorious with potential in the face of that truth.

I was theirs, and through their possession, more my own than I was anywhere else.

My womb was contracting hard enough to send tears to my eyes, and my body was trying to curl in on itself, trying to survive the onslaught of sensation crashing through me. My thighs were tight and straining, the cuffs were digging into my wrists and ankles, and the throbs surging from my clit outward to every part of my body were agonizing and wonderful.

And then the moment the orgasm began to ease, the stranger's hands moved. A slender hand pressed above my belly button, joining Rafe's hands in holding me still, and then I felt an unfamiliar sensation against the taut muscles of my lower hole. The stranger was rubbing me there, and then with a finger lubricated with my own slick, I was slowly, inexorably invaded. All while the stranger's hot mouth nursed on my clit, flicking their wicked tongue over the sensitive bud protruding from under my hood.

I couldn't tell where the first orgasm ended and the second began, but it didn't matter, nothing mattered except Rafe and the stranger and me, and I was nothing but theirs, nothing but mine, and I'd been born to feel this, made for the sole purpose of feeling their ownership, right here, right now. The sensation crashing through my body only confirmed this, *affirmed* this, etching me from the inside out with that indelible truth.

I was theirs.

I was theirs.

And I wasn't sure whose name I said first as I came, but I knew that I said both—keened out a hoarse *Lox, Rafe, Lox. Rafe.*

Whether or not Lox was actually there didn't matter, because she was there *to me*, she was there in my mind, taking this from me. Giving this to me.

It wasn't until Rafe's hands loosened on my waist and the stranger pulled away that I realized I was sobbing, trembling, a ruin. The stranger's orgasms had wrecked me, and I didn't know that I ever wanted to leave the rubble they'd left behind.

"I think we all know our winner, then," Rafe said, and I was distantly aware of laughter, whistling. "Everyone, please applaud our victor. Robin Loxley."

EIGHT

LOX

I IGNORED the applause and stared across Marian's trembling body to the wolf on the other side.

"Congratulations," he said softly. "You won the game."

The inside of The Knot was like the inside of a ruby—dim and red and glinting—but even if it were midday in the desert, I wouldn't have been able to decrypt Rafe's expression. *It's a trap,* Jovanna had warned me when Much Miller had called to tell me about the game Rafe was playing with Marian. *It's a trap and she's bait. And you know it.*

Of course I knew it. But traps only worked if one got caught—and I wasn't planning on getting caught. The actual problem was that I couldn't be sure what trap Rafe had actually laid, and his demeanor right now gave nothing away. He looked for all the world like a cool, cruel dominant, pleased with his sub's performance, and utterly in control of what would happen next.

But there *had* been a moment—blurred by lust and motion and urgency, to be sure—when he'd been holding

Marian down and I'd been eating her cunt and our eyes had met and...

And *what*, I didn't know. Only that we could have been in Carpathia all over again, meeting for the first time, the spy and the mathematician-turned-soldier-turned-spy. Ice and fire and power and desire; an inevitable but addictive disaster.

"What do I win?" I asked, sweeping my tongue over my lower lip. Rafe's gaze followed the movement and then flicked back up to my eyes. My lips tasted like Marian. He knew it.

"Name your prize," he said. "I'll decide whether or not I want to give it to you."

I broke our stare to glance around the club. Much was here, and I'd brought Will too, but if there were agents here aside from Rafe, it wouldn't have made a difference. I hadn't brought Much and Will to fight, only to keep an eye out for me.

I saw nothing suspicious, and when I looked back to Rafe, he was as unreadable as ever. Surely if he was planning to pounce now, he'd be tense, exhibiting constant awareness, trying to herd me somewhere?

"I want to help with aftercare," I said, and the facade cracked the tiniest bit at that.

His eyebrow lifted. "Aftercare," he repeated. He didn't sound happy about it.

He wanted to keep Marian to himself.

And after watching him tonight, the way he touched her, savored her, held her down, I had the sick feeling that his motivations toward Marian were getting murkier by the day. It would be unforgivable if he used her for intelligence, to get to me.

But if he fucked with her heart? Her happiness?

I would kill him. I'd kill him and toss him and his ridiculously big watch into the Pacific.

After a long moment, Rafe gave me a nod. A sharp one that let me know that I'd gotten to him with this request, and that he was only acceding reluctantly.

Or that's what he wants you to think.

It didn't matter. Me and the data were safe either way. It was Marian I was worried about.

I gently pushed the blindfold to Marian's forehead, my chest constricting at the soft, owlish way she blinked up at me. She was gorgeous and mussed and marked all over, and still cuffed and spread like this, she looked like a wet dream brought to life. I wanted to keep her cuffed here forever; I wanted to grab her and haul her back to my forest to be my queen fox once again.

"It's you," she said in a dreamy murmur. "I hoped it would be."

I brushed my finger over her cheek. Her face was exquisite. I wanted to bite it.

"It's me, little fox. I'm going to uncuff you now."

Rafe had already started on her ankles, and I made quick work of her wrists. Without asking me, he gathered her in his arms and lifted her off the platform. Last time I'd seen Marian in Rafe's arms, she'd looked like a freshly ravished bride. Now, with her red dress and well-bitten neck and breasts, she looked like the victim of a particularly pervy vampire. Or a pack of pervy vampires.

"Lead the way," Rafe said with her in his arms, and because the crowd had begun to disperse around the stage, it was easy enough to steer them down the stairs to the far hallway and to an open private room beyond.

Rafe followed me inside and kicked the door shut behind him. He strode forward with his usual decisive stride, walking towards me and the bed with Marian tight in his arms, her hands laced around his neck and her hair hanging down in glossy, tangled waves.

My heart gave an abrupt lurch at the sight, and then a breathless squeeze. Like a giant fist was inside my chest, quashing and crushing the organs there like so much pulpy fruit.

I was jealous, I knew I was jealous, but it was jealousy *and* something else, and it felt horrible and mouthwatering all at once.

Seeing them together, walking toward me, felt like being awake after years of being asleep. It felt like that first painful breath upon breaking the surface after a deep, deep dive.

I closed my eyes, and when I opened them again, Rafe was helping Marian onto the bed. She looked completely wrecked, a thoroughly used submissive, and yet her eyes were bright and her mouth was curled in a dazed smile. Like the other night, she was still deep in subspace, but tonight she seemed more limp and happy than kink-stoned out of her mind.

"You can leave now," I told Rafe as I approached the edge of the bed.

"Oh, I'm not leaving."

Fuck me, he was infuriating. "You said I could name my prize. I named aftercare."

"Should have read the fine print, Lox," he replied crisply. "I never said you could claim your prize alone."

We glared at each other a moment, until Marian pushed up to a sitting position. "Is there any water in here?" she asked, and Rafe and I turned toward her, both of us looking guilty. We should have gotten her something to drink the moment we walked in, we should have made sure she was seen to before we fell into another one of our pointless sparring matches.

"Yes, darling," Rafe said. He went to a narrow closet and opened it; inside there was a small fridge and built-in shelves stocked with everything someone could possibly want after a scene, from personal wipes to Clif bars, and he grabbed a small carton of water from the fridge along with personal wipes and an ice pack. When he returned to the bed, he set the wipes and ice pack down on the silk sheet, and then opened the carton of water for Marian to drink from.

I couldn't help but watch as his long fingers made deft, efficient work of opening the cardboard. As he held the carton to Marian's lips for her to drink.

By the time she'd finished, I was handing her the wipes so she could clean her well-used sex. The wipes were cool, and she shivered a little as she wiped the insides of her thighs too. As she cleaned, I checked the red-blooming bites and bruises to make sure there wasn't any broken skin or deeper contusions. She'd only be a little sore tomorrow.

Sore enough to remember me, but not so sore she'd have to abstain from play. Exactly how I liked it.

"Show me your breasts," I said, getting a fresh wipe from the container.

Rafe tugged down the bodice of her dress before Marian could comply, and as irritated as I was that he was still here, I couldn't deny that it was helpful to have an extra set of hands to help with aftercare.

I also couldn't deny that the sight of Rafe's hands hooked around the red silk of Marian's dress sent abrupt and contradictory things blowing through me like gusts of hot, dangerous wind.

Marian hissed as I used the cool wipes on her breasts,

all shivers and goosebumps as I cleaned her, and when I finished, her nipples were pulled into tight little points that I couldn't resist rolling between my fingers.

"What do you like in your aftercare?" I asked, because I had to ask. Because I'd never given her aftercare before.

Because the one time I should have, I left to go to war instead.

Marian stretched a little, her bodice still tugged down and her gown still shoved up around her hips, her hair more tangled than I'd seen it since we'd spent hours and hours playing foxes in the forest.

She looked beautiful like this. My wild fox, unburdened from whatever it was that had made her so cool and closed off over the years.

"I like to be held, I think," she said. "But I don't know though, this is still new to me—"

I was already reaching for the cashmere blanket folded neatly at the bottom of the bed and wrapping it around her. I then crawled onto the bed behind her and pulled her into my arms and between my legs, settling in with her back to my chest and her head tucked under mine. I folded the ice pack into the blanket so that it would be nothing more than a whisper of coolness and then slipped it between her legs to rest against her pussy.

Marian raised a hand to Rafe, her meaning clear.

She wanted him on the bed too.

I wanted to kick my heels against the bed in protest; I wanted to snarl and snap at the wolf in our room until he slunk off. I wanted Marian to be mine and only mine—and I certainly didn't want to share her with an ex-lover who'd chosen a country over me—but unlike Rafe, I was cuffed and bound to the truth. To what I believed the truth demanded of our actions.

And tonight the truth was this: Marian wanted Rafe here.

RAFE LOOKED DOWN at Marian's outstretched hand and then up to me, his pale eyes betraying nothing of what he was thinking. But I saw the muscle jump in his jaw, the slight twitch of his hand at his side. For the first time tonight, including as he'd watched me grope and bite his new submissive, he looked uncertain.

I gave him a small nod to indicate I wasn't going to argue. I was certain all the reluctance I felt was showing on my face right now—but I dearly fucking hoped none of the other unwelcome feelings currently twisting inside my chest would reveal themselves. I didn't want them to exist; and if they absolutely had to exist, then I didn't want Rafe to know about them.

Rafe climbed easily onto the bed and sat next to me, so very close, close enough that we touched.

He had to, I knew, in order to be close to Marian. In order to touch and kiss and stroke her like she so clearly wanted. And yet it had the effect of pressing his entire body flush to mine, all the way from our feet to our hips to our shoulders. And I'd forgotten how firm his body was, how layered with muscle it was, how warm he'd always felt, always, even in the middle of a Carpathian winter that could freeze the tit off a witch.

I'd forgotten his scent too. It had always smelled like money to me—literally like money. Like walking into a bank, like pouring coins onto a table, clinking and spinning, like the crisp five dollar bills my grandmother used to press into my hand whenever my parents weren't looking.

It shouldn't have smelled as good as it did, but there

was something so sharp and clean about it, something so ruthless and also yet so reassuring. His scent was certainty itself. Or at least as close as any scent could come to something like that.

"Thank you," Marian said, her voice falling into a soft moan as Rafe took her hand and began massaging it. She made the noise again as I began stroking her hair, slowly and carefully unknotting it with my fingers. My free arm was wrapped around her waist, and my thighs cradled hers.

At the bottom of the bed, combat boots and gleaming Oxford shoes and dainty bare feet splayed on the sheets in a strange array.

My throat hurt to look at it.

"How did you know about tonight?" Rafe asked after a moment. His hands were so gentle with Marian's hand as they massaged. It was almost impossible to believe that just half an hour ago, they'd pinned her to that platform so I could finger her ass to my heart's content.

"A friend," I said. He didn't need to know that Much Miller was the club's manager and also one of our Merry Men.

"Ah," he said.

It's a trap and she's bait. And you know it.

"Were you expecting me to show up?" I asked, watching his hands carefully work all the tension out of hers. I couldn't ask what I really wanted to ask, not with Marian listening—and I could tell she was listening.

I didn't blame her. I'd listen too if my two ex-lovers were propped together in bed behind me.

"I suppose I imagined it was a possibility when I planned tonight," said Rafe.

"Because I can't resist a challenge?"

"Because you're an incurable show-off," replied the spy.

"An impulse one might think would be curtailed by running from the government, but alas."

"I'm not a show-off," I said, a little moodily. "I just know when I can win things, that's all."

"Wait," Marian said from in front of me, "so Rafe knows you're hiding from the FBI too?" She twisted a little, but she couldn't twist enough to get a good look at his face. "Did they also come interview you, Rafe?"

"The FBI interviewed you about Lox?" Rafe's voice was neutral, but I wasn't fooled. I'd heard that neutrality in Russian, in Portuguese, in Pashto, in flawlessly accented French. I'd seen him maintain that neutrality in deserts, half-abandoned outposts, in cities so crowded that every movement had to be planned days in advance. He cared very much about this, and there was no reason I could discern other than that he cared about Marian.

But could I trust that about him? Trust that he'd put Marian first if it came down to it?

"They did, about a year ago," Marian said. "Lox thinks she's protecting me now by not telling me anything about where she's been or what she's been doing. I don't even know where she's staying while she's here."

"She's protecting you," Rafe said. "As I would do."

"Are you...agreeing with me about something?" I asked, turning to look at him. "Is this a Christmas miracle?"

Rafe finished massaging Marian's hand and began stroking it instead, caressing her with lingering touches that were no less measured or methodical for their tenderness. "We had a few things we used to agree on, if you'll recall."

Before you turned traitor seemed to be the unspoken coda to that.

"Like kink," Marian said. "You were kinky together. Right?"

"I don't think *kinky* is the right word," said Rafe, the neutrality exchanged for dryness now. "Warlike, maybe."

I scoffed. "You're being melodramatic."

"I? *I* am being melodramatic?" Rafe gave me an incredulous look. As if to say *coming from the woman who stole state secrets and claimed it was for the greater good?*

Marian had settled back against my chest again, sighing as Rafe's fingers moved up her arm. "But it must have been good sometimes. Otherwise you wouldn't have stayed together at all, for any length of time."

Rafe and I didn't answer that.

Because yes, it had been good sometimes.

"Do you miss them?" she asked. "The warlike parts, I mean?"

Rafe's fingers hesitated where they were caressing her. "This is a strange conversation to have, Marian," he said.

I had to agree.

"Maybe," Marian said, "but all of this is a little strange, don't you think?" She gestured to the bed, to us tangled together in our red silk and imported wool and tactical nylon. "What about this is an ordinary kind of night?"

Next to me, I felt Rafe's chest lift in a subtle but long breath.

"Why do you want to know?" he asked after a minute. He wouldn't look at me, even when I looked over at him, and it suddenly felt like my ribs had contracted inward on themselves, like there wasn't enough room for my lungs to pull in the air they needed. So I held Marian a little tighter, like I could possess her thoughts by sheer proximity, like she could possess mine in return. Like she could crowd out the lingering memories of anyone else—specifically the memories of a certain half-British spy.

"I don't have a reason other than curiosity," she finally answered, her voice soft. "When I think of you two together, I'm jealous and curious and...and I don't know. Greedy for both of you. Greedy to know everything about you, even if it's about how you loved each other before now."

The word *loved* was like a gunshot in a closed room, a lethal crack through the air, leaving blood and plaster dust in its wake, and I closed my eyes when I heard it.

Loved. Yes. I'd loved him.

If I was being honest, I loved him still.

Rafe had frozen next to me—even his hands on Marian's arm were utterly motionless—

and just when I thought he would say nothing, when I thought the moment would die the death it should have died before it was even born into being, he spoke.

"Yes, Marian," answered the wolf. "I miss them."

I looked at him and he looked at me.

"The warlike parts," he said, his gaze not leaving mine. "The wrong parts. I miss them all."

His eyes were hooded, his long lashes draping his eyes in shadows upon shadows, and I'd forgotten what it felt like to have all that lupine attention on me, all that dangerous hunger settled on *me*. It made me want to growl and bite, to take and chase.

Not to warn him off, but to provoke him into growling and biting back.

"I miss them too," I said in a low voice.

"But you left," said Rafe.

I drew in a shaky breath. "Well, I'm back now."

He was closer now—or maybe it was me who was closer, maybe it had been me who'd pressed in, who'd sought the ghosts of his exhales on my lips. Maybe it had been me, and maybe leaving had never mattered, because leaving only changed where you were, not who you were, not whom you loved, and maybe it was some kind of sick fate that I'd end up right here with Marian and Rafe. Feeling Marian in my arms and Rafe's breath against my lips.

Now it was him who drew in the shaky inhale, and then it was our mouths brushing once, twice, before finally connecting in a searing slash of want. Rafe couldn't even kiss without reconnaissance, but I couldn't be mad about it, not when his lips were as warm as his kiss was demanding. I met him back, matching demand for demand, until he relented and let me push my tongue between his lips.

He groaned as I did so, and Marian was twisting in my lap, and Rafe's fingers were in her hair and also fisting in my leather jacket at the same time. The stroke of his tongue against mine was like gasoline in my blood, accelerant on a bonfire, and his scent was all around me, crisp paper and hard metal.

A rough hand shoved itself down the front of my pants, finding my clit with unerring accuracy—and Marian's soft mouth was all over my neck as her hand joined Rafe's—and he was hauling her closer—and for a single tangled and panting moment, everything was perfect.

Perfect.

It didn't matter that Rafe was a dominant, that we could only kiss and grab and fuck as some sort of twisted battle of wills, because Marian was between us, absorbing pinches and squeezes and bites with delighted sighs. It didn't matter that Marian was never supposed to want this, because she'd already proven that she did want it, and she'd wanted it enough to find it without me. It didn't matter that I wasn't supposed to be here, that I shouldn't be with them at all, much less crossing all the boundaries there were to cross, because the only thing that could ever matter was this filthy and long-denied kiss.

The only thing that could ever, ever matter was the three of us: the thief, the maiden, and the wolf.

It took me far too long to become aware of Jovanna speaking into my earpiece—her low voice had been drowned out by the gasps and groans and the feeling of Marian softly, but with admirable expertise, edging me toward a massive release.

"Lox," Jove was saying in my ear. "Lox, did you hear that last part? Zhang is *there*. He's there at The Knot. He's at the bar, and Will says there're three cars in the parking lot that are coming back with cloned registrations. Which means you need to get the fuck out of there. *Now*."

It only took two heartbeats for Jovanna's words to process. One heartbeat to hear. Another heartbeat to understand.

I've been set up.

Jovanna had been right all along—tonight was a trap and I'd swallowed the bait whole. In front of a crowd no less.

I shoved myself back, getting myself off the bed in a few fast, sharp movements. Both Rafe and Marian blinked at me with pupil-blown eyes, their lips wet and swollen, both of them visibly and obscenely aroused.

I was shaking, and to my eternal shame, it was only half from the fury and adrenaline of realizing I was about to be captured.

The other half was utter longing to be back on that bed.

"I knew it," I whispered, my voice trembling with anger as I took another step back and tried to take stock of my options.

"Knew what?" asked Rafe, looking genuinely confused.

"That this was a trap. That you set me up. And now—" Fuck. I didn't have time for this. I needed to get the hell out of here, I needed to get to my bike before they figured out it was mine. Unless they already knew, which would mean making it to the backup location on the beach so one of the others could get me...

How could he do this?

And how could I have been so stupid?

"A trap?" Marian asked as her gaze slid between the both of us. "What are you talking about?"

"It's not a trap," Rafe said slowly, as if he finally understood what I meant. "Give me some credit, Lox. We've discussed this already. Getting you here at The Knot would hardly serve my purposes."

"Discussed *what*?" asked an exasperated Marian. "What purposes?"

I looked over to her, and whatever resolve I'd had to keep her as non-complicit in this mess as possible blew away like leaves before a storm. She needed to know, because if Rafe was closing in on me, then I couldn't trust that he wouldn't close in on *her*, and after our little show tonight, we were past the point of ignorance keeping her safe. The entire club had seen me wringing orgasms from her, and more importantly, they'd heard her scream my name. They'd watched as the three of us went to a private room. The NSA would be very interested in that. And *interested* in this context could be extremely dangerous.

And anyway, I'd want to know if a lover were using me as leverage. I was sure she would too.

"He's been lying to you," I said finally. I glanced over to Rafe, who was motionless on the bed, his pale eyes glittering. His hand was still tangled in the silky fabric of Marian's dress. "He's here in Sherwood for me. To...apprehend me."

Marian laughed, a musical sound at odds with the urgent truth poisoning the air in the room. "He's with the EPA, Lox. They don't arrest people."

"He's not with the EPA," I bit out. "He's not here for whatever reason he told you. He's here for me. He's using you to get to me. Whatever is happening between you two is a lie, Marian."

Rafe remained still, but Marian drew back, getting to her knees on the bed as she looked at him. "You're not— this is about Lox?" She shook her head. "No. No. That can't be right."

The burning rage I felt toward Rafe did nothing to muffle how much it hurt to watch Marian realize the truth. To watch her shoulders curl in and her head lower as Rafe said, "It's true, darling."

But neither did the burning rage harden me against the relief I heard in his voice, against the tender, almost remorseful shape to a mouth that was normally such a sharp and vicious cipher. As if he were grateful he didn't have to lie anymore.

"He's working with the NSA," I said, shaking it off. I didn't have time for Stockholming. "And he has people here in the club tonight."

"Lox," Rafe said, straightening up and lifting his hands, as if to show me he had nothing to hide. "I'm not going to take you here at the club—"

"Another car's just arrived," Jovanna said in my ear.

"We're waiting for the registration to come back, but the three dudes climbing out of it do not look like they're here for kink. They look like they're from the IRS with the awful suits they're wearing. Jesus."

I believed it. The NSA had branches that were trained for covert ops, but most NSA and CISA employees were techies and data-crunchers. It could be the FBI—I rather hoped it was the FBI, since they were a thousand times more likely to do everything by the book—but either way, I had to go.

"Come with me," I said urgently to Marian. "Please."

"That's not necessary, Marian," Rafe said. He still had his hands lifted, palms out, fingers up. A quelling gesture. "I'm not going to let anything happen to you. And nothing is going to happen to Lox right now."

"How can I trust you when you've just admitted that you've been lying to me? When you told me you'd tell me the truth always?" she asked. She blinked furiously, as if refusing to let a single tear fall. "When you've just admitted that all of this has been about getting to Lox?"

"Because, I—" Rafe stopped, his jaw tight. "Because everything else between us has been real, darling."

Marian looked down again, sucking in a deep breath.

"Lox, you need to *go*," Jove said in my ear. "The IRS dudes are coming through the front door now. You can still make it out the back if you hurry."

"I'm not going to stop you from leaving," Rafe told me. "But taking Marian with you is dangerous. You know that."

"More dangerous than her staying with you?" I demanded. "Where you can fuck with her head some more, maybe have her detained to lure me back out again?"

Anger—real, cold anger—flashed across his face. "Your

opinion of me is quite clear if that's what you think I'm capable of."

"My opinion is formed by your actions," I said. "Or have you forgotten that you tried to kill me?"

"You tried to kill me first, as I've already made clear," he said tightly. "And I wasn't trying to kill you, I was trying to stop you."

"By killing me." I didn't have time for this. I walked to the bed and held out my hand for Marian to take. "Your choice," I told her. "Come with me or stay with him."

"And if I go with you?" she asked. "What does that mean? For me? For my work?"

I shook my head slowly. "I don't know, Marian."

"You won't have committed a crime by going," Rafe said. "But if you learn of treasonous actions wherever you're at, then you risk becoming complicit in the government's eyes. At the very least, you risk being brought in for questioning once we find you again."

"And if I stay, I won't be questioned?" Marian asked.

Rafe shook his head. "I can't promise that."

At least he was being honest. "If you stay, you will be watched," I told her.

"If you go, you will be hunted," countered Rafe.

She looked down at her hands, which were fisting and rubbing the tops of her thighs. "I can't make a decision this quickly," she breathed.

"Then don't," Rafe said. "Stay. Take time to think about it. If you still want to run off and play Robin Hood with Lox, then you can later."

"He's lying, Marian," I responded quickly. "Later is too late. The choice is between you *having* a choice and him using you. The NSA watching you. For the next decade at least, you will be on their radar, and that's the *best*-case scenario. *Please*."

She looked at him and then at me.

She took my hand.

"Don't do this, darling," Rafe said, and I knew I wasn't imagining the pleading in his voice. "Don't."

"I'm sorry," she whispered. "Sir."

LOX

Jovanna was talking in my ear as I led Marian to the back door of the club. "There's no one in the side lot where you've parked your bike. Much Miller says no one's come close to it, so I think we're fine when it comes to trackers, but I still think you need to take the long way to the castle just in case."

"Copy," I said, tugging Marian along behind me. She was barefoot and mussed, and I didn't even know what we looked like, with me hauling her off to places unknown while she was shoeless and well-fucked, but at the very least, it wouldn't look out of place at The Knot.

And anyway, it felt right to do. Right to finally, finally take her to the world I'd built. Marian would be my queen fox after all.

I kicked open the back door, scanned the empty lot, and then lifted Marian into my arms without asking.

"Lox," she protested, squirming.

I held her easily, although I still walked quickly toward

my MV Agusta parked in the far shadows of the lot, because I didn't know how long I could hold her if she really wanted to fight me on it. "I don't know how much time we have," I said. "Bare feet will slow you down. Here."

We got to the bike, and I set her on her feet before reaching for the helmet I had strapped to the back.

"No," she said when I tried to hand it to her. "Don't you need one too? I can't take the only one!"

"Not up for debate," I told her tightly, guiding the helmet onto her head before she could try to argue any more about it. After that came my jacket, which luckily she accepted without a fight, and then I pulled the tangled silk of her hair out from under its collar. I mounted the Agusta, kicked up the stand, and pulled the key out from a chain around my neck. After the bike roared to life, I tilted my head at the seat behind me. "Get on, Marian."

She didn't hesitate, but it was obvious from the careful way she straddled the seat that she'd never ridden on a motorcycle before.

"Hug me tight," I told her, and despite everything, my heart flipped sideways at the feel her hands sliding around my waist and pulling herself close. "Lean when I lean. Tap my arm if you need something."

I felt her nod against me, and then I peeled out of the lot, checking behind me to make sure we weren't being actively followed.

Nothing but empty streets and the flapping of Marian's red dress behind us.

"Make sure you're taking the long way home," Jovanna reminded me in my ear. "Just because they're not following you directly from The Knot doesn't mean they're not still following you."

Amen to that.

We sped south, quick, zipping onto 101 and flying as fast as we could away from town. To my right, the ocean was an endless black stretch beyond a thin screen of fir and pine. To my left, Sherwood Forest was a canopy of shadow, a playground of night, home. I couldn't wait to get back.

But first, I had to make sure the wolf wasn't on our tail.

We wound south for a long time, turning off onto smaller and smaller roads, until finally we were moving north again—albeit north in the most indirect way possible. The breeze as we rode was damp, cool, and Marian snuggled even closer, her chest to my back and her thighs framing mine. I imagined I could feel the heat of her bare cunt behind me. I wanted to taste it again so much that it was like a physical ache in my bones and in my belly.

You can once we get to the hideout, I bartered with myself. We'd have all the time in the world there, and no more secrets between us.

It took us more than an hour to get to the abandoned farm that marked the starting point for the path home. There was no road beyond the edge of the forest, not even a gravel one, but the narrow trail that wound through the woods was perfectly clear and firm once you got beyond the deadfall disguising its entrance. Soon the farm was no longer visible behind us, and we were deep in the heart of the forest, ribboning through cedars and hemlocks and dodging the moss-covered fingers of the wood as we went.

And then we were there.

I slowed the bike to a crawl and tapped my earpiece once. "We're home," I told Jovanna. "No one followed us."

"Copy that, fearless leader," Jovanna said cheerfully.

"Why have we stopped?" asked Marian, her voice muffled by her helmet. She hadn't relinquished the death grip she had on my waist, and I found I didn't want her to. Ever. "There's nothing here."

To the untrained eye, there *was* absolutely nothing here. Nothing other than a fast-rushing stream that had carved itself a steep cleft in the soil and rock and then the rustling ghosts of the trees around it all. It looked like any other patch of Sherwood Forest, untouched and utterly uninhabited.

"Watch," I told Marian, and then a narrow moss-covered door slid back to reveal a concrete ramp lined with dim red lights.

She let out a long exhale behind me. I smiled.

And together we rode into the Castle of the North Wind.

"So your father built this place?" Marian asked after emerging from the bathroom in a pair of my briefs and a T-shirt. As much as I enjoyed the red dress, I didn't think she'd want to meet everyone in the clothes she'd just gotten publicly railed in.

I handed her a pair of sweatpants, shamelessly watching the plump curves of her ass as she pulled them on. "When I was a child. He was—he had these phases, you know. These moods. Times when he'd spend every waking hour restoring an old boat, other times when he'd go to Mass twice a day, and then other times that were packed full of too many obsessions to keep track of. He had enough money to indulge in any whim he wanted, no matter how ridiculous, and that's how the castle came to be. An underground bunker invisible to the outside world, so it could withstand the collapse of society from...well, from climate change or a solar flare or whatever crisis he was obsessed with at the time. It sat empty for years after he finished it."

"Until you needed it," Marian finished for me.

"Until I needed it. It was perfect for us, you see, because it was built for hiding. And it was more than large enough for all my rigs. All I needed to do was fortify the HVAC to accommodate my machines, make sure that thermal output was well-masked, and I was ready to go. Oh, and get secure internet, but building secure communication systems in risky places was literally my job for the NSA, so it wasn't too much trouble."

Marian wandered around my bedroom, trailing her fingers over the concrete walls and built-in bookshelves—stocked almost entirely with paperbacks from fifteen years ago. Relics from when my father had the place built.

"I was still a kid when he passed, and so I hadn't realized he was so..." She stopped, obviously looking for a polite word.

I gave her one, although I privately had lots of better words. "Eccentric? Intense? Yeah." I looked at the room, at the physical manifestation of millions of dollars poured into a single person's temporary obsession. "It was hard on my mom, I think."

"Was it hard on you?" she asked, turning to face me. "That kind of intensity?"

It would be easy to say yes, I thought, easy to translate my father into some sort of symbol for capriciousness or neglect, but that *yes* wouldn't capture so much of what Robert Loxley had been. Ready to act, ready to leap. Like the fool from the tarot deck, already stepping off the ledge with his face to the sky.

Land or sea? Dad asked me once, when I was twelve, standing on the beach by our house. *If you had to pick.*

Both, I'd said immediately, not even stopping to think about it.

He'd laughed. *That's not the point. You have to choose.*

Well, that had just been stupid. Who said I had to choose? The rules of some choosing game he'd literally just made up? Why did I have to agree to play at all? And anyway, I couldn't have picked between the two if I'd wanted to. The sea was a vast cold salt full of cruelty and life; the land behind me was a nest of trees and stone and moss, all of it draped in fog like the tattered veil of a dead bride.

I loved both; I'd have both. No one could force some bullshit choice onto me, not even my own father.

Both, I'd said again, stubbornly. *You can't make me choose. I won't do it.*

He'd smiled then, one of his wide, half-wild smiles. The kind my mother used to tell me I'd inherited from him. *That's my daughter*, he'd said, eyes twinkling. *Never, ever let anyone make you take less than what you want.*

"Not like you're thinking," I said finally. "It wasn't easy sometimes, but he always gave me what I needed." I waved at the room around us. "And he still is, even though he's gone."

Marian dropped her hand from the bookshelf and stepped toward me. "I'm glad," she said quietly. "I'm glad you've had someplace safe to hide."

My chest ached. I didn't deserve that from her, not after the way I left things.

Marian's gaze moved past me, and then something flitted over her face, soft and almost wounded.

"My ribbon," she whispered.

I turned to see what she saw, and yes, there was her hair ribbon from that fateful day, tied in a neat bow around one of the rails that made up my headboard. The ends were ragged and fluffed where the weft had slowly unraveled through years of handling. That ribbon had gone everywhere with me, into combat with me, on missions so dangerous that I wasn't even allowed to wear American clothing while I did them. That ribbon had been to hell and back with me.

Even Robin Loxley wasn't brave enough to visit hell without a piece of heaven nestled close to her heart.

"I didn't know," she said, sounding stunned. "I had no idea."

"I told you, Marian. I remember that day so well, it hurts. Come," I said, swallowing down the ache and taking Marian's hand. Her fingers were cool and slender in mine, and I felt along the contours of her knuckles with my thumb. Every part of her was so exquisitely made, like porcelain and silk, and all I wanted was to shove her against the wall instead of taking her to see the rest of the castle and its crew.

Alas.

"Let's meet everyone," I said with heroic self-restraint, and with hands linked, we left my room.

CHAPTER
TEN

The Castle was the size of two or three warehouses laid side by side, divided into the three more or less similarly sized pods. One pod was a storehouse—food and other supplies were kept there, along with our miniature water and wastewater treatment facility—and the next was our living quarters, which was a ring of bedrooms surrounding an open central area with a kitchen and common space. There was also a gym, a pool, and a small first aid center. The final pod was where we stored the rigs and we usually kept it closed off from the rest, since the machines gave off so much heat.

I was still in my clothes from earlier, and my boots thudded on the polished concrete as we walked into the common area. Half the people in the room were hidden behind triple monitor setups and desks piled with energy drink cans.

"These are the Merry Men," I said, waving at the room's

occupants, who didn't bother looking up from their screens when they waved back.

"Merry Men?"

"When my dad built this place, he called it the Castle of the North Wind—what Robin Hood called his hideout in my favorite childhood stories. And Will and I realized that *we* were the Merry Men now, in our own Sherwood forest. We're not bandits or deer poachers, of course, but we are stealing. We are hiding."

Marian's full mouth pressed in at the corners. "It fits, I think."

"You don't even know why we're hiding here yet. For all you know, it could be exactly as Rafe said."

"Treason? I don't think it's that...at least not simply that. I trust you, Lox."

Like it was just that easy. Like she could just trust that I was a good person and trust that my reasons were good ones, and that was the end of it.

I blew out a long breath, looking down at our interlaced hands. I hadn't realized how much I needed her belief until I had it. Because maybe my father had been able to subsist on his own delirious convictions alone, but I couldn't. People saw me and thought they saw unshakeable faith, absolute certainty, and that wasn't *always* wrong.

Maybe it wasn't even wrong most of the time.

But the times that I did feel doubt, disquiet, wavering... those times *infected* me. All of me. Like a multipartite virus, overwriting and rewriting everything I thought I knew with bedrock certitude, erasing any confidence I had and planting new code in its place. Code that said: *you're wrong about what you've found*, code that said: *you should have gone to someone with this.*

Code that said, *you're going to be locked away forever and so will your friends...and that might even be the best possible outcome of this gamble.*

I didn't know what I would have done without the crew, without their clear-eyed faith. Without their confirmations that they were seeing what I was seeing, without their agreement that the things we saw couldn't stay as they were.

But having Marian look at me like this, clear midnight eyes and open trust, felt better than anything. Better than the time we came to the Castle and realized we could hide here indefinitely. Better than when I passed Ranger school, than when I graduated from MIT. This felt like maybe— *please God, maybe*—everything might be okay.

Because with her by my side, how could it not?

"And who is this beauty I see?" A tall, fair man with rakish hair and a lip piercing came from the kitchen, his arms outstretched, and Marian let go of my hand and ran straight for him, burying her face in his chest as he gave her a massive hug. She probably hadn't seen Will Russo since he left for college, but six or seven years had nothing on a childhood of summers spent together in the forest.

"I didn't know you were back," Marian whispered, hugging him tighter.

Will squeezed her. "It had to stay a secret, chérie. And now you know why."

"Chérie?" Marian asked, pulling back to look at him. "Are you French now?"

"You haven't heard?" Jovanna asked as she approached. She had deep umber skin, long box braids, and a recon squadron insignia tattooed on her bicep. She still had something of the Army about her—a warm geniality for those she considered family along with a muscled frame, perfect posture, and abrupt transitions into bluntness.

"Will paid for that fancy college in Zürich by flogging French housewives over his term breaks. You're looking at the one and only Monsieur Scarlett, one of the premier doms of the Paris kink scene."

Will made a face as Marian laughed. "Thanks, Jove. Would you like to tell her about my internet search history too? Maybe what brand of condoms I use?"

Jovanna gave Will a look. "She just came from The Knot. I don't think your flogging fame is going to bother her. And also hi, I'm Jovanna," she added, turning to Marian and extending a hand. "Lox and I were the only two women in our Ranger school class, and we were inseparable after that. She couldn't shake me even after she went rogue."

"Not that I tried too hard," I said. In addition to being one of my closest friends, Jovanna also had a knack for surveillance as a former drone operator for the Army. She'd been the subject of many recruitment attempts—mostly from intelligence agencies, but also from the private sector —but she'd stayed Army until the day she left.

Left because of me. Left *with* me.

"Are Tuck and Much back?" I asked Jovanna, and she shook her head.

"They stayed in Sherwood to keep an eye on Rafe and Zhang," she said, and I could sense the question coming before she asked it. "And why isn't Rafe chasing you right now? Why didn't he grab you while you were there?"

"Maybe it wasn't a trap?" Marian said, hope lining the insides of her words.

Jovanna gave Marian an appreciative glance, her eyes moving from Marian's bare feet to the ponytail currently swept over a slender shoulder. "Sweetheart, he made you both the game *and* the prize. He might as well have sent a hand-lettered invitation to my friend over here."

"I'm not that predictable," I cut in, but Jove just rolled her eyes.

"You should have seen this dummy in the Army," she said to Marian. "Every single time there was a contest—rope-climbing, push-ups, who could eat the most DFAC Popsicles without throwing up—your Lox was right there in the thick of it."

"That's because I knew I could win," I said, a little grumpily.

"You lost that push-up contest, *and* you couldn't move your arms for a week after. And I've never seen an ass-chewing like the one you got after you and Johnson polished off half a freezer case of Popsicles and he puked orange goo all over your CO's boots. So I don't know if I'd count that as a win."

"Plus tonight was about *Marian*," Will said, and Jove nodded in agreement.

"And Rafe de Lacy," she added, "the only other person who redirects all the blood from Lox's brain to her sex parts."

"Erroneous. He also sends blood to my strangling and clawing-his-face-off parts."

"I see that you're not fighting me on the sex, though, and that's very wise of you. Also we still haven't satisfactorily answered why Rafe and Zhang didn't just take you while you were there."

I rubbed at my eye, suddenly and overwhelmingly exhausted. "Lackland wants the machines, not to mention all of you. And Rafe knows we have contingency plans for the stolen data if I'm captured. I know he's waiting for leverage, but I thought..."

"That I was the leverage?" Marian asked. When she looked at me, I saw too many things in her face to name.

I nodded.

"Right. So here's the way it should have gone: he uses Marian to lure you to The Knot, and then detains you," Will said. "Makes you think that he still has Marian, even if he doesn't, and uses that threat to extract our data Plan B out of you. It would have worked, because you charged right into his trap like a maniac, but he didn't do any of that. Why?"

I kept rubbing at my face until it hurt. Until it felt like I could push my fingers all the way through my skull and agitate my brain until it worked as quickly as I needed it to.

"He must have a different plan then," Marian said. There was a briskness to her words that didn't feel entirely like corporate efficiency. More like she was forcing herself to accept a very jagged truth. "At The Knot, he said Lox was safe right *now*. It was intentional wording, like he already knew exactly what he was going to do."

"Don't be moody," Will said, looking at me.

"I'm not being moody."

"You *are*." He looked over to Marian. "She's the moodiest. Do you remember this? The goddamn moodiest."

I threw up my hands. "I'm only moody when it's called for! Like when the NSA is *here* and waiting for us to fuck up!"

"The good news is that you know those assholes, and you know how they think," Will said. "And we've already dodged them for a year. We'll be fine."

Jove stared at him. "I think *fine* might be stretching it."

I agreed. Will didn't know Rafe like I did, and I knew he hadn't made a mistake tonight. Maybe the private room hadn't been part of the plan, but it hadn't hurt his plan, whatever that was. Even Marian coming with me hadn't seemed to bother him in any capacity other than as a dominant and a lover. Which meant she wasn't essential to what came next.

"Now that we've gone over the whole being hunted part," Will said, "have you told our fair maiden the good news?"

"There's good news?" Marian asked, a winged brow lifting high. I could imagine her giving someone in a boardroom that same expression.

"Yes," I said, grabbing her hand again and pulling her. "The good news is that you're now among the best and cleverest thieves in the world. Come on."

Passing by a few of the others still behind their computers, I gave Marian their names—Alana, Doncaster, Bland, and Tinker—and then explained that the latter three were hackers Jove, Will, and I had recruited in our first month on the run. Alana had come on board as our machine expert, and then when we returned to Sherwood, I reached out to Tuck and Much, both of whom worked in private cybersecurity, to join us. Together, we'd formed the Merry Men, stealing from the government to—hopefully—find a way to fix it.

Not that we knew the best way to do that.

Even a year out, we were still divided on how to use what we'd stolen.

But I wasn't going to worry about that right now.

The first thing that hit us when I pulled open the door to the last pod was the warmth, a thick blanket of it settling over our shoulders as we stepped inside, and then the near-darkness, filled with thousands of blinking green and red lights. Our footsteps echoed on the perforated flooring as we walked down the central aisle. Rows and rows of black shelves housed CPUs and GPUs capable of ingesting, processing, and storing data, their cords bundled in neat black and yellow twists, their fans whirring silently. The nearby air-conditioning units were caught in a continuous, throaty roar.

Marian came to a stop, blinking as she looked around the room. I could see the lights from the rigs caught in her dark eyes. They sparkled like stars.

"What are all these?" she asked over the noise of the air conditioners. "What are they for?"

"Secrets," I said simply. "Secrets that we're not supposed to have."

Her lips parted as she put it all together. "This is the treason?"

"In a loose sense, yes," I said. A red light flashed nearby, and Will and Jove walked over to check it out. The sensor lights for that aisle kicked on as they approached, and in the new glow, I could see the glittery sheen of sweat misting on Marian's neck. I wanted to lick it off. "It'll be easier to explain if I start from the beginning."

"A long story, then?" she said.

I smiled and somehow managed to drag my eyes up from her lickable throat. "It's actually not as long as you might think. All told, it took me less than a day to decide what to do. But it still wasn't an easy decision."

Ahead of us, Jove and Will were poking at the rig, Jove's long braids and Will's floppy hair waving from the drafts created by all the whirring fans.

"At first," I said after a minute, "I thought they were mistakes. Errors. Something getting fucked up in the ingestion of data. Rafe and I were partnered together in a few different regions to plant secure communication and listening devices in neutral or hostile territory, and so it was my job to get those systems up with very limited time and under significant pressure."

I still remembered installing surveillance equipment and their upload links in a block of flats in Carpathia, a river town called Bassas that had been mostly blasted to bits during the war and hadn't been rebuilt since. Even though the new Carpathian president Svenchenko had managed to bring some semblance of stability to the country, the extremists proved especially stubborn to root out, and were under our constant surveillance. Bassas had been a hotbed of radical activity at the time, and I'd installed the equipment while Rafe stood with his back to mine, his hand on a gun with the serial number filed off. We'd made it out of the building, but then got caught by rebels at a checkpoint on the road and had to shoot our way out. It had been the first time I'd fired a weapon since leaving the Ranger battalion, and I'd been sick after, throwing up the moment we'd stumbled to safety in an abandoned gas station. Even now, I couldn't tell you why.

"So at first," I went on, "I thought maybe I'd fucked up. That the data had gotten...I don't know, compromised or corrupted in such a way that would make it look like what I was seeing. And then I double- and triple- and quadruple-checked, and no, the equipment was fine and the algorithms securing the information were fine. So then I wondered if it could have been intentionally planted misinformation. But no. It was all verifiable."

Will and Jove walked back toward us, the aisle lights shutting off behind them, leaving us in the eerie glow of the rigs.

"We're going to make grilled cheeses," Will said. "Do you want any?"

"Maybe later," Marian said politely.

"Your loss. I make them the French way."

"And what does that mean?" I asked. "You sing Patrick Bruel to them while watching a depressing movie?"

"I put *ham in it*," Will said, affronted, and then left us with a very Gallic sniff. Jove followed, giving us a wave as she went.

Marian turned to me. In the low light of the room, I could only make out the implication of her face in the dark. A full mouth, high cheeks, an upturned nose. All of it bathed in a green, almost forest-like glow.

"What was all true, Lox?" she asked, returning to what I'd said earlier. "What did you see?"

ELEVEN

LOX

"A message from John Lackland to someone in the Carpathian government. *Proceed. For Ys.* That was all it said. The next day, three American birds were blown up on a Carpathian base. No injuries, but millions of dollars gone up in a plume of smoke." I sighed. "Rafe thought I was seeing something that wasn't there."

"But I couldn't stop thinking about it," I continued. "The timing, the sign-off. *For Ys.* It didn't take being a cryptographer to know that meant something. So I did what I wasn't supposed to do, and I started searching more of Lackland's messages, not just from that data lake, but from other lakes as well. And like I said earlier, I thought I must be wrong, or that I'd fucked up the installs, or *something*, because the more I searched, the more I found shit that shouldn't be there. Burner phones, addresses, money transfers. And those were enough for me to find what really mattered."

One of the big fans at the end of the room began rotating slowly, sending puffs of air down the central aisle.

"And here's what matters: there is a global network that operates on a scale you can't imagine, and has for...well, for longer than I think it's possible to prove. It's called Ys, and its members are politicians, religious leaders, military leaders, businesspeople, and people you've never heard of and never will. It is almost entirely invisible, entirely made up of whispers and ghosts, but their hand is in everything. Our largest decisions as a country—wars, sanctions, legislation—are filtered through Ys."

Marian was staring at me, and I gave her a sad smile.

"That's the same expression Rafe wore when I told him."

"Is this the night you tried to kill each other?"

I sighed. "I wasn't actually trying to kill him. Just make him...well, sit *down* for a moment so I could get away. But yes. It was that night."

"Did you decide to run before you talked to him?"

I closed my eyes. "Do you think you can be loyal to your country even as you're committing treason? Do you think that you can serve a country you're stealing from?"

"Yes," Marian said softly. "I do."

I opened my eyes. "Rafe didn't," I responded. I was proud of how level I sounded, how unwounded.

"Categorical good and bad applies to so many things, but I don't think loving a country is one of them," she said, and I was so goddamn relieved to hear her say that.

"But why haven't you gone public with it yet? That's what whistleblowers do, right? They blow the whistle for other people to hear?"

"Yes," I said. "They do."

"Then what are you waiting for?"

An excellent question. One with no answer—at least no agreed upon answers among the Merry Men. "Jove and Tuck want to wait until we have more before we release it to the press. They think the more damning it all is—the sheer amount of material we could have if we waited—will make what we've found impossible to ignore. Which is sensible, given how improbable this whole thing is. Will and Much want to move faster. We can always release more as we get it, but in their view, if we don't act now, we risk getting caught and not able to release anything at all."

"Surely you agree with Will?" Marian asked. "Acting fast, that's usually your style, Lox."

I didn't like hearing this. Not because it hadn't been true in the past, but because I worried that it was no longer true. That I'd lost some essential character trait in the last year—that I'd lost hold of some indelible *Loxness* that made me who I was. That I'd become slow, overly careful, and that

somehow, in following what I believed more empathically than I ever had before, I had become less like myself.

It was an uncomfortable feeling. A lonely feeling, except the loneliness wasn't located in being alone, but being separated from the oneness I used to feel inside myself.

"I don't want to fuck it up," I said finally, the admission coming out in such a low voice that Marian moved closer to me to hear it. "All my life, I've been like my father, stepping off cliffs and leaping and grabbing at what I wanted. MIT, the Army, Ranger school...working for the NSA. I never stopped to wonder if I was doing the right thing, because it all felt right. It all felt necessary. But now—well, this might be the most important thing I ever do, and both options feel right, so how do I know which one to choose?"

Land or sea? That was what my father had asked me, but

I wished I could ask him what to do when the choices necessarily excluded one another. Act now and tip our hand, or wait until we had a stronger position...but possibly miss our chance.

And the stakes were too high to choose wrong.

Marian reached for my hand, and I took it, seized it.

"You'll choose the right thing," she whispered.

"You don't know that."

"You always have."

I shook my head, slowly, the heat inside my chest matching the warmth of the computer farm behind us. "Not true. I left you."

I could see her swallow, the subtle shift of shadows in the dark, and then I was walking her back to the wall next to the door, back, back, until she was pushed up against it and my hands were planted on either side of her head.

"What's your safeword?" I asked, running my nose along her jaw, smelling her, sweet sugar with just a hint of the sea.

"Red," she said, lifting her chin for me so I could more easily reach her throat.

I kissed the damp skin there. "Unbutton my pants," I told her. And then said, when she obeyed, "Good girl. Now unzip them."

The zipper was thick and sturdily made, and each metal tooth made a heavy click as the zipper pull moved down, down toward the bottom stop. The endless breezes and sighs of the computer pod wafted more warm air against my already warm belly; I could feel, with subatomic precision, exactly where the band of my underwear stopped and where my skin began. I could have measured down to the micron where Marian's hands were in relation to my navel, to my cunt.

I could have calculated the time it would take for her to slide her hand down the front of my underwear, and I would have been exactly right, I would not have introduced a single millisecond, microsecond, nanosecond more.

I still didn't know how much experience with kink Marian had, but she knew enough to keep her hands where they were, one on the fabric of my pants, the other on the tab of the zipper, waiting for her next instruction.

I licked her throat and then said, "Let's put those pretty hands to good use, Marian. I want one on my cunt."

She shuddered out a breath, her lids going heavy as she did as she was told and slid a hand down my belly, past the wide elastic at the top of my briefs. I grunted when I felt the first graze of her fingers—grunted again as they moved over the stiffened flesh of my clit.

I widened my stance, boots heavy on the perforated metal floor, and gave her more access.

"Clit now," I told her. "You can play later."

She nodded quickly and used two fingers to circle and stroke. The climax was already gnawing at the hollow places of my body, desperate to claw its way out. The first time I had Marian touching my cunt in five years, and I was about to go off like a teenager fooling around in the back of her car for the very first time.

I dropped my head back and blinked up at the dark ceiling above us, searching for control, needing to make this last.

The high, narrow slits in the ceiling—made in the earth above the pod and fringed with ferns and moss—betrayed the occasional wink of stars through the trees, and I tried counting them, I tried breathing to the rhythm of the counting, but it was useless. I'd been wet and needy since the club, since licking Marian's sweet pussy, since feeling

Rafe's mouth on mine as his hand twisted in the leather of my jacket—

I moved my head forward and bit her neck, her jaw, her lips. She was perfect, so she let me, she let me kiss and lick and bite, giving me gorgeous little sighs as I did, her braless nipples poking through the loose T-shirt like hard little bullets. I reached down and cupped her pussy, feeling the heat of her even through the sweatpants, wondering if she was sore from earlier tonight, wondering if I could make her give me just one more release...

"Lox," she said. I could feel her breath on my lips...and the submission in that one syllable alone was enough to undo me. My clit felt like the center of universe, her fingers too, but also her mouth and her eyes and her fierce, beating heart, because she'd always been fiercer than me, because she'd been willing to stay, stay when it was messy and hard and heavy. All I'd ever done was flee to thing to thing to thing.

"I can feel how wet you are," she whispered, and even though she was only rubbing my clit, I was moving against her enough that things were slippery enough that she had to focus to keep her touch right where I'd commanded it.

Soreness be damned, I tugged down the waist of her sweatpants and found her sex, the shock of hot, swollen skin against my own enough to make me growl. She was wet enough that I didn't have to go searching for it, slick against my hand, and I bit her throat again as I came with a rough, urgent noise.

I came like I hadn't come in so very long, since Rafe, and it felt like a fire tearing through me, like the end of all things was happening right in the center of my body. Convulsions rippled out, *lashing* out, hot waves everywhere, and I could barely breathe for it, I could barely survive it. But if I didn't survive, this was the way I wanted to go: with Marian's cunt in my hand, my mouth on her neck, her fingers between my legs.

Her breath and the hums and breezes of my stolen treasure mingling in my ears.

The clenching waves emanated and then abated, slowly, waves on an ever steeper shore, and at long last I could lift my face to hers and see those eyes shining with the lights from my rigs.

"You did so good," I told her, and she bit her lip in a shy smile.

"Thank you," she said, and I kissed her.

"Tell me," I said against her lips, my fingers running through her slippery need, "if you're still at—"

"Green," she said, before I even finished asking. "Green green green—"

The first blare of the alarm was loud enough to make us both startle. I looked around, my hand still firmly between Marian's legs, and then the alarm screamed again, this time with bright, blinding flashes of light.

"Fire?" Marian asked.

"Maybe," I said. Although I worried it was something even worse. I pulled my hand free and helped her dress, but there wasn't any time to button my own pants before the door to the pod slammed open and the Merry Men poured in.

"Proximity alarm," Jove said over the alarm. Her expression was grim. "They're outside the ramp right now, figuring out how to get inside."

I swore, stepping away and then turning back again. "How many?"

"Six or seven. If it were a siege situation, we could outlast them for months. But if they figure out a way inside

—one of the egress tunnels maybe, or through our water system—we're screwed."

Will approached, looking like a sketch in the harsh strobe of the alarm. "Just say the word, Lox, and Plan B can happen right now."

"I need a minute," I said tightly, trying to think. Could Rafe find a way in? How long would it take for him to guess the size of the castle, to hunt for its years-old permits and permissions? The electronic records I'd destroyed a long time ago, but there might still be paper records, and he'd need only wait for daylight to go bother some county clerk for them. Shit.

I looked at them, my Merry Men and my Marian, all of them watching me with faces full of trust, of readiness. They would do whatever I suggested, and the responsibility that came with that trust could crack my bones if I let it.

But there was no choice. Not really. There was no sense in making a stand that risked the brilliant, brave people in front of me.

And Marian...

No. Nothing bad could happen to my queen fox.

"Plan B," I said. "We turn this into a furnace and run. We meet at our usual spot by dawn."

"But—" Marian looked around at us. "The data you took, that you're storing—you can't mean to destroy it? After everything you've been through?"

"We have a backup data farm," Jove assured her. "It's not nearly as big as this one, we're still working on it, but we always knew this might be a possibility. Besides, it gives us more reasons to spend Lox's weird dead dad's money. No sense in it languishing innel secret offshore accounts forever."

"Okay, everyone," I said. "We have fifteen minutes. Let's turn off the alarms, get our shit, and start a fire."

"And then get the hell out of here," Will said with a salute.

"And then get the hell out of here," I agreed with a half-smile, and we scattered, me pulling Marian along as I half jogged back to the central pod.

Once in my room, I got her a pair of boots, tossed her my leather jacket, and then started shoving my laptop and tablet into my bugout bag. Within just a few minutes, the alarms were blissfully silenced and we were ready to go. Marian and I went back out to the common area to look at the surveillance feeds while everyone else finished closing up shop.

Sure enough, there were people tramping outside the castle with flashlights in hand and cellphones pressed to ears. When I finally caught sight of Rafe's broad, suited shoulders and angular face, I felt like I'd been kicked in the stomach.

He looked up at the camera I was currently using to watch him, mounted outside on a tree, and he stared for a moment, as if holding my gaze through the feed, even though he couldn't possibly know I was there. As usual, his face was impossible to parse, and just when I was about to look away, I saw his mouth move. Two words.

I'm sorry.

Chills ran down my spine, down every nerve to my fingertips and the bottoms of my toes, and the same chill was inside my chest and my throat.

It shouldn't *hurt* this much to be betrayed by Rafe de Lacy again.

And yet.

"How did he find us?" Will asked, coming to stand next to me in front of the security feeds. "It must have been a planted tracker, but Jove and Much swear no one came close to your bike."

"I don't know," I said. My voice sounded thin after the klaxon shriek of the alarms. "This is hardly a place anyone would stumble upon by chance, but the only thing he could have tracked was my bike, because I brought nothing else inside the club..."

I stopped. I'd brought nothing else inside the club—except for myself. With a sick, miserable clench in my stomach, I turned to face Marian, who was wearing my leather jacket, and I slipped my hand into the inside pocket.

I found it right away.

A black disc about the size of a quarter, but flexible around the edges. A green light blinked at the top.

The memory of Rafe's hand fisting my jacket as he kissed me, of him pulling me closer while he waged war on my mouth, burned through my mind.

Betrayed with a kiss. And now my own personal Judas was outside the gates to finish the job.

I set the tracker on the desk and found a piece of paper, and wrote a little note to Rafe about what he could do with the tracker once he found it.

"Wow," Will said. "That's creative. Even I've never heard of that, and the dungeons in Paris are *wild*, I mean wild like you wouldn't believe—"

"Are we ready to go?" I asked him as I straightened up and tossed my Sharpie back on the desk. If Rafe charged in here, I hoped he found the note. I hoped he knew that *I* knew when he'd planted it on me. I hoped he hated himself for it.

"All ready to burn, my friend."

I nodded, shoved down the sick, shivering hurt, and grabbed my bag. "Then let's go."

"Okay, but important question first."

I looked at him, my hand laced in Marian's and my bag over my shoulder.

Will gave me a very serious, very intense expression as he asked, "Are you ever going to button up your pants, because it's very distracting, and I think it'll impede your—"

That almost pulled a real smile out of me, and I shoved him. "Let's go, asshole."

With only a few keystrokes, the rigs had begun to shut down, and they were dying as we walked into the computer pod and then to the far end, where the three egress tunnels led out to the forest.

The mood was quiet but not overly grim as we made our way to the tunnel entrances; this wasn't ideal, but we'd planned for it. The data would be safe, we'd be safe. We had a place to go and, because of the family money I'd secreted away, more than enough to keep the Merry Men and our dream going.

I looked back at the aisles of now-dead CPUs and GPUs as the others started filtering into the tunnels.

I'm sorry, Rafe had said into the camera.

Had he been sorry even as he'd kissed me? Even as he'd searched out my cunt with his fingers and held Marian close so we could both play with her?

Marian squeezed my hand now and I swallowed. In less than an hour, this room would be charred metal and concrete, pools of melted plastic and fumes. We'd be on a beach, having taken different routes out of the forest, planning the best way to get to our backup location on the other side of the state. And the Castle of the North Wind would be a burned and empty ruin. A dream that ended with two words.

I'm sorry.

I turned and led Marian to the tunnel entrance. We were the last ones to leave and I made sure to shut the door behind us.

IT TOOK us hours to carefully and quietly make our way from where our tunnel dumped us to a road, and then from the road to a small beach nestled directly underneath the cliffs my childhood home rested on.

The house had been sold right after my mother had died—I had no use for a too-big mansion while I was in the NSA anyway—but there was a narrow path to the beach that was hidden from view, and the beach itself was impossible to see from the house above. Unless someone came by boat, we were invisible.

As the sun heaved itself up from the forest to our east, we began to take stock, to make sure we were all okay and had everything we needed to run.

Except—

"Where's Will?" I asked, stepping to the side to make sure he wasn't slouched on the sand somewhere. "Has anyone seen him?"

They shook their heads, and that's when Alana and Tinker stepped onto the beach, their clothes muddy and their faces full of shame.

"They were waiting outside our tunnel," Alana whispered. "We tried to run, but..."

"Where's Will?" I asked. The panic was a cold collar around my throat. "*Where is he?*"

"I think they got him," Tinker said miserably. "He was

running with us, and then he wasn't, and when we looked back, we could see their flashlights..."

"You weren't followed here, were you?" Jovanna asked urgently.

They both shook their heads.

I looked at her and Marian. "Rafe has him," I said. "I know it."

"Lox," Jove said. "Let's not do anything rash. Please. We still don't know."

But when I looked at Marian's face, I could tell she knew what I knew. Rafe knew I had some sort of contingency plan for the machines, he knew there was only one way I'd ever break.

I'm sorry.

I sucked in a long breath, looked down at my trembling hands. Curled them into fists.

I'm sorry.

Was he? Was he really?

I remembered the way he looked at Marian last night, his pale eyes softer than I'd ever seen them. *Everything else between us has been real...*

And the thing was that I believed him. I believed he cared for Marian. And I...I even believed that he was sorry.

Not that it made me want to strangle him any less.

"I'm open to any non-rash ideas," I said finally. "But you only have the next twenty minutes before I do something rash anyway."

Jove groaned. "Please don't tell me that you already have a plan."

"Then I won't," I said. And then I squinted at her. "Which is probably a good thing, because I can promise you'll extra hate this one."

RAFE

"You can't make me talk," the young man said, pushing me out of my thoughts and back into the present. I walked away from the exposed balcony and into the tarp-strewn shell of the unfinished house, stopping once I reached the feet of Will Scarlett. He was currently zip-tied to a folding chair, his ankles also bound together, and the breeze blowing in from the window openings lifted the mud-matted hair off his face.

He glared at me as I squatted down to look him in the eye.

"I don't need you to talk," I said simply.

"That's bullshit," he spat, all bravado, all fear. Lord knew how he'd managed to fool all those French kinksters into thinking he was mature enough to be a dom. "I know what you want. You want me to give up everyone else, and Lox besides, and I'm not going to do it. And I'm certainly not going to help you sift through all those charred CPUs back in the forest to look for clues."

I held up a hand. "Allow me to stop you, Will. I don't need your help with charred anything, much less a list of your associates. I only need you to be here."

He struggled against his bonds a moment, before slumping back. "What are you going to do to me?" he asked, the defeat evident in his voice. "Are you going to kill me?"

"I'm not even going to keep you here after I'm done with you," I assured him, standing up. "Once Lox arrives, you're free to go."

The millionaire who'd tried to build this house had gone bankrupt halfway through construction, and the structure had been caught in some sort of asset limbo ever since. Since it was isolated enough that sound wouldn't carry and far enough away from the road that any comings and goings would go unnoticed, it made a very convenient interception point for Lox.

Will lifted his head to look at me. The gray light of morning kept the night shadows close. They wreathed around the doorways and crawled along the legs of his chair. "I don't believe you," he said.

"You don't have to believe me," I said, walking back over to the balcony. Built into a jut of earth deep in the forest, the balcony opened onto the trees themselves, and I could see the rivers of morning fog as they moved over the forest floor below me. "But that doesn't make it any less the truth."

"You're not any less reprehensible for it, you know," he said fiercely. "Using me to get to her is even worse."

"Do you know why we're alone right now?" I asked. I turned and braced myself against the balcony's railing as I looked back at him. I knew I looked like as much shit as he did—I hadn't slept, my suit jacket had long been abandoned, my trousers were wrinkled, and my shirtsleeves were rolled up to my elbows. I didn't even know where my tie was.

"Because you lied and you're actually planning to kill me?" he said, again with that shaky bravado that made him look so young, so very young.

I ignored his accusation. "Because I know Lox, and I know that she will come to find you. And when she does, I will let you go, and then I will convince her to do the right thing before Zhang and the others have a chance to get involved."

"You're deluding yourself if you think Lox will ever choose to betray us. No matter how convincing you are. No matter how *alone* the two of you are."

His conviction shone through almost as much as the fear. "You really believe her, don't you? Believe that Ys exists?"

"Belief isn't required," Will said. "I've decrypted this shit myself. It's all real, it's all documented. How can you not believe her? When you can see the evidence with your own two eyes?"

I didn't answer right away, and maybe he was a better dominant than I'd thought, because he found the thread of my thoughts more easily than he should have.

"Ahh," he said softly. "So that's why we're here—why you want Lox alone before the others can get to her. You want to hear what she has to say. Maybe you've been watching Lackland over the last year and wondering if the idea of Ys isn't so far-fetched after all."

I knew my face betrayed very little, but for the first time in a long time, it was a near thing. Because he was right. He was right, and I didn't know what to do with all the doubts swirling inside my thoughts like so much mist creeping over the sea.

When I came to Sherwood, I knew the job. I knew the target and I knew the stakes. Lox was a traitor and had to be stopped.

But the Lox I'd encountered had been the furthest thing from the Lox I'd constructed in my head since she'd left me a year ago. I'd forgotten how brightly she burned, how cleanly, like the flame off a candle, the edges as sharp and clear as her mind.

In my memory, it had been easy to turn Lox into something other than what she was—too eager to believe, maybe, or too stubborn to change her mind, or too idealistic to accept that no reality was a perfect moral landscape. But that wasn't *her*, that wasn't the actual Lox. The actual Lox wouldn't chase a fantasy, and she certainly wouldn't risk her friends and Marian for the sake of her own stubbornness.

And I still loved her.

As good at my job as I was, I couldn't pretend that away.

My phone buzzed, and I pulled it out of my pocket to answer it, walking into a different part of the empty structure so Will wouldn't hear my conversation.

"She's approaching," Zhang said. "You were right. She took your bait immediately."

"She won't want to waste any time," I murmured, pushing aside a tattered plastic sheet to peer down the dirt road leading to the house. I'd texted her where I was with Will only an hour ago, guessing that what I'd said to her about Marian would hold true for her childhood friend too.

Love seeded lapses in judgement. Love begetted mistakes.

Whether it was old love or new love, lover-love or friend-love, it was all the same. Good people would risk everything for it, and despite what Lox believed of herself—despite what I'd used to believe of her—she was a good person. Chaotic maybe, and reckless, certainly.

But good.

"I'll be sending Will Scarlett out once she gets here," I told Zhang. "You're to let him go, unfollowed."

Zhang made a noise. "Lackland won't be happy about this. You know he's on a plane to Olympia as we speak, right? He wants Lox and everyone and everything associated with her, and he wants it off the books."

Off the books was not good. Off the books meant no written reports, no memos, no records.

My hand tightened around the phone, and I forced myself to sound even and calm as I said, "I still need three hours, Zhang. Just give me three hours before you let him or any of his personal jackals up here. I think I can get Lox to turn on her own, and you know that if she does, the quality of intelligence we'll get will be so much better than if Lackland throws her into a cell somewhere and subjects her to the worst shit he can think of."

"I'm just saying that I don't know if I can hold him off if he gets to Sherwood faster than we plan, okay? I've never seen him this intense about literally anything before."

Because if Lox is right, this information could destroy him.

"Fine," I told Zhang. "But at least promise me nothing happens to Will Scarlett."

"Nothing happens to Monsieur Scarlett," Zhang said with the gusto of someone who'd had way too much fun reading Will's file. "Scout's honor."

"And make sure none of Lox's people come up here either. The last thing I need is some sort of rescue attempt derailing everything."

"We'll watch the perimeters, but you know as well as I do that this environment is porous as hell. I can't promise anything."

"I still appreciate it, Zhang. Thanks."

I hung up, and as I dropped my hand to my side, I saw her. She'd changed into another pair of tactical pants, a dark gray this time, and she wore a thin ribbed tank top without a jacket. Her dark copper hair was tousled on the side where it was longest, and without her usual lipstick, her face looked open and young. A woman in her mid-twenties who loved combat boots and the forest she'd grown up in, nothing more.

I greeted her at the yawning concrete mouth that served as the structure's entrance.

"No jacket?" I asked.

"Some asshole put a bug in it," she said, walking right past me. "Where is he?"

"Just ahead."

I followed the heavy tread of Lox's boots on the unfinished concrete, and I saw her shoulders slump with relief as she saw that Will was here and indeed unhurt. She turned to me. "Are you really letting him go?"

I pulled a small knife from my pocket, and with a few tidy movements, Will was free and on his feet. He scowled at me as he rubbed his wrists.

"Come on, Lox," he said, his voice low. "We can leave right now. Together. You don't have to stay."

Lox's green eyes flicked over to meet my gaze, and then she shook her head. Slowly. Almost sadly. "No, Will. You go. I need to stay."

"You won't be followed," I said to him without taking my eyes from Lox. "I give you my word."

"That means fuck all coming from you," Will said, but Lox just gave him a look.

"*Will*," she said. "I need you with the others, do you understand? For whatever might come next. They'll need you. Marian will need you."

Will softened a little at that, but he still gave me a poisonous glare. "If anything happens to her on your watch, I'll make sure you die a miserable death."

It was a threat I'd heard thousands of times before, but this morning, it had some sting. Everyone assumed I wanted to hurt Lox, make her suffer, and it was starting to wear on me.

I just wanted her safe, *and* I wanted my country safe, *and...*

And...

And I didn't know what either of those two things meant anymore. Definitely not in conjunction with one another.

With a final, reluctant look at Lox, Will went out the entrance and down the dirt track through the trees, his shoulders hunched and his head swiveling from side to side, as if expecting an NSA agent to pounce on him at any moment.

Once he'd disappeared from view, Lox turned to face me, her jaw tight.

"So I'm here," she said. "What do you want with me? You want to humiliate me before you detain me? You want a little light interrogation before Lackland gets his hands on me?"

"I wanted to say I'm sorry," I said quietly. "For Marian. For last night."

Her lips pressed together before she spoke. "You told me that love would lead me to make mistakes and you were right. I was so certain that you were using Marian against me that I didn't even see the catch and release. Lure me in, bug me, and let me go. You didn't need me to talk or confess, and you didn't even need me zip-tied to a chair. I led you right to the castle all on my own."

"It was a brilliant place, Lox," I said softly. "I was sorry to see it burn."

"I'd be a fool to believe you."

"Even so. And I'm even sorrier about Marian," I told her, taking a step closer. "Bringing her into this was fucked up, and now she's part of it all, and I never wanted that. I only wanted to get close enough to you to get what I needed for the job."

"And now you've cornered me. For what? For me to cooperate? Because that's what this is, isn't it? You thought if you could get me here by myself, I'd fall prey to those pretty eyes and give you everything you want?"

"I don't know," I said, and it was the truth. "I don't know what I'm thinking anymore."

She stepped forward too, distrust written all over her face. Distrust and anger and every simmering feeling that had always been between us, ever since the beginning.

"Am I supposed to believe that Rafe de Lacy is growing a conscience?"

"I've always had one, Lox. You don't have a monopoly on giving a shit."

She was close enough now that she had to tilt her face upward to look at me. "So what are you saying, then? You're choosing to give a shit about this?"

I ran my hand over my face. "I'm saying that I'm willing to listen to what you've found."

She scowled, her soft mouth turning down at the corners in the way that I'd always found so adorable. It made my cock hard. "This is an interrogation tactic."

"It is," I admitted, "but it doesn't have to be only that. I —" I stopped. I couldn't finish the sentence, not yet, because I didn't even know what I wanted to say. *I think you might be right.* Or *I want you to be right because I still love you.*

Or *I want to fix this because the thought of never seeing Marian again feels like a flogger snapping against my naked heart.*

"If you were me," I said quietly, "what would you say? What would you do right now? Lackland is on his way to Sherwood. Zhang and the others know you're here. This is supposed to be the end of your Merry Men. *I'm* supposed to be the end of it. So what is it that I should do?"

"You're an asshole," she said. "I hope you know that. You're asking me what you should do when you're the one with all the power here, when you're the one who manipulated me here in the first place."

"I don't know how to tell you any more clearly that *all* the choices are extremely limited right now, yours and mine. So if you'd like anything different to happen other than the inevitable, I need your help."

"This feels like another interrogation tactic, and *God,* I wish we could just try to kill each other again, that was so much easier than this."

I sighed. "I wasn't trying to kill you. But if you'd like to fight me again, you're welcome to try."

Her eyes narrowed; her tongue pressed against the tip of one of her sharp incisors. "Or maybe I should try punishing you instead. Any hard limits, Rafe?"

"Treason. Why don't you at least tell me what you think can be done about Ys, and I promise to listen."

"That's not why I came here," she said, stepping close enough now that her boots crowded my dress shoes.

I looked down at her. Green eyes, dark red lashes. Beautiful, half-feral features. "Then why did you come here?"

"For this," she said, and then her fists were in my shirt and her mouth was on mine.

The shock kept me still, and it was *shock*—shock like I'd never felt in combat or in danger. Shock like my entire body was made of nothing but blood and heat, made of nothing but the mouth currently slanted against hers and the cock straining against my fly.

I found her waist, grabbed, and she twisted her hands in my shirt and pulled. We fought, half grappling, half stumbling, until I was able to slam her against one of the bare walls of the structure and pin her there with my hips.

She hissed as I palmed her breast over her tank top and then shoved my hand up her shirt to do it again. Her fingernails raked through my hair, and I felt her broken exhales against my lips as I found the buckle of her belt.

"I have to fuck you," I grunted, and she bit my ear in response.

"I know."

Her belt fell free, and then I worked mine open with one hand, my other hand sliding through her copper hair and pulling until she growled and bit me again.

I spun her around, and she was already guiding her knickers and trousers over the tight curves of her ass as I did, never one to let me have the lead for long. It made me hungry, eager, the kind of hungry and eager that felt almost angry, but deliciously so, and I sank my teeth into her shoulder as I unzipped my trousers and pulled out my dick.

She was wet—nothing made her wetter than fighting—

and after a perfunctory check with my fingers, I pressed the head of my cock to her opening and wedged my way in.

"Fuck," she moaned, pressing her face against the wall. "Rafe."

"I know," I said. My jaw went tight and every muscle in my body clenched as I pushed all the way in, deep enough that my hips were flush to her ass and every inch of me was buried. Her cunt was a hot, satin glove—just the slick squeeze of it alone was threatening to undo me—and how I'd lived without this for the last year, I had no idea.

True to form, Lox tried to take control right away, bracing her hands on the wall and fucking herself back on me like I was nothing more than a dildo suctioned to a mirror. But with her trousers and knickers binding her thighs together, there was only so much she could do, and I relished that, that accidental bit of bondage and the way it made everything tighter and sweeter and rougher.

I slid my hand around her waist, which gave me the dual pleasure of getting to fondle a breast and also restraining her a little, so I could hold her still enough to properly fuck her. She squirmed and struggled against me, not to get away, but to fuck me harder than I could fuck her, and the noises filled the hollow space: slaps of skin, the rustle and pull of fabric, hoarse grunts and low moans.

I found her clit with a hand shoved between her thighs, and gave her the firm circles I knew she liked, two fingers against the stiff bud.

She arched this way and that, as if not sure exactly what front she wanted to battle me on, and I laughed as I kept screwing her.

"You fight even when I'm inside you," I grunted, "and I can't tell you how fucking hot it makes me." I was hard enough that it *hurt*, even inside the wet silk of her.

She reached back and found the nape of my neck, her fingers twisting in my hair until I hissed. "You never fight hard enough back," she mumbled. She was still trying to take over, rolling her hips to meet mine, bucking against my fingers on her clit.

"Last time I did, you accused me of trying to kill you."

"So I have a flair for the dramatic."

I pressed my lips to her ear. "I'm fucking you against a wall when I should be dragging you back to the NSA. Is that dramatic enough for you?"

"Make me come, and then we'll see," she dared, but it was an empty dare, and she knew it. She was closer than I was, judging by her moans and the shivering, writhing state of her, and it only took a few more hard thrusts for her to grunt out my name and then seize around my erection.

I swore, rutting even rougher, savoring each and every cry of hers, each and every flutter around my cock, and then with more profanity tumbling from my mouth, I came, flooding her with my orgasm and shuddering in the sweet, wet relief of it all. The relief of having her as mine once more—even if it was only for a few desperate minutes against a wall.

Even if it was only for as much time as it took to come to our senses.

We separated slowly, reluctantly, as if neither of us wanted the spell to end. I flinched as I pulled free of her pussy and the cool air of the room hit wet skin, and I was half tempted to shove back inside and stay there until I was fully hard and ready to fuck again for real. It wouldn't take more than a minute.

Lox did that to me. Made me insatiable.

She turned, buttoning up her pants, and I did the same as she spoke in a low voice, "Thank you."

"For fucking you?"

She looked away. "Stop it."

"Then *you* stop it. I'm the one who's been missing you —hurting for you—wishing I could find a way to stop loving a woman who couldn't give a single shit about me."

She looked incredulous. "Is that really what you think? That I don't care about you? Rafe, I *love you*, and God knows why, because you are everything I shouldn't want to love."

My hands froze on my belt.

"You love me?" I asked. The words came out as query and accusation both—hopeful and bitter.

Lox stepped back toward me, her expression fierce. "I never stopped, Rafe, just like I never stopped loving Marian."

"I never stopped either," I said. "But I think you already know that. Don't you?"

Her teeth scraped over her lower lip as she held my stare. And then she nodded. Once. "I think I do."

And somehow this was more intimate than what we'd just done against the wall. More urgent, more naked and vulnerable even than sex.

"I love you," I said. "I love you so much that it scares me, because sometimes I think that I don't believe in anything more than I believe in you. Because...because sometimes I think if I had to live through the night you left all over again, I would come with you rather than spend a single moment apart ever again."

She swallowed.

"There it is," I said, giving a laugh that wasn't really a laugh at all. "I hadn't even admitted it to myself until now. But it's true. I can't bear to lose you again, Lox. I thought it was the only way last time; I told myself I had no other choice. But I'm done with any choices that aren't *you*."

A tear caught on her eyelashes, and she blinked it away, her mouth trembling. "I want—I always wanted you by my side. When I first met you, I knew that I was supposed to spend the rest of my life fighting with you, trying to tear you open the way you tore at me, and leaving that behind hurt more than almost anything else." She drew in a quavering breath. "If you want to see what we've found out about Ys, then I can do better than tell you. I can show you. But not here."

"Lox, we can't leave. There's a perimeter around the house—"

She looked at me like I was being intentionally thick. "This is Sherwood, Rafe. *My* Sherwood, and I know it better than anyone. I can get us out without being seen. The question is will you come with me? Come all the way with me?"

My hand found her waist, her hair. She pressed her body against mine, her lean curves flush to my frame, and I remembered how it felt in that bed at The Knot, her and me and Marian, tangled together, Marian's surrender like a shared banquet between us.

"Are you asking me to leave my job behind? My life?"

"You don't have a life," she said, and I gave her a dry smile, because she knew me too well. Even my apartment in D.C. was little better than a hotel room, where I kept my clothes and books, and little else. There wasn't time or energy for domesticity with my job, and I was home so rarely that I didn't even keep anything but baking soda in the fridge. It would only take a call to a donation center and a cancelled lease to erase Rafe de Lacy's "home".

"Fine. But my country? I'll be a traitor too."

Her gaze was steady, even with the tears still wetting her eyelashes. "If we do this right, we save the world from

Ys. Which means that if we do this right, we might be heroes."

"I'm not a hero, Lox."

I knew what I was. I knew what I'd done and what I was capable of doing. There was a reason that half the work I'd done over the years was classified, and that the other half hadn't ever been committed to writing in the first place.

Lox tilted her head up. Her eyes glittered with something almost like mischief. "Well, I'm definitely not. I'm something much better."

"And what's that?"

"A thief."

I PRESSED my forehead to hers and wondered if this had been inevitable all along.

From the moment I bit Marian's wrist.

From the moment I saw Lox on our first mission in Carpathia, all green eyes and sparks of fire.

Lox found my hand, laced her fingers through my own. "Marian's waiting for us," she murmured. I opened my eyes and looked down at our hands.

"You think—the three of us—?"

"We've seen it work before, haven't we?" she said. "President Colchester, his First Lady, and his Vice President —if the rumors are to be believed, they made it work too. Why not us?"

"One, because we'd be on the run from the entirety of the United States intelligence apparatus. Two, because you and I are only capable of eating each other alive."

"But maybe she was what we needed all along," Lox said as she searched my face. "The two of us together— we're like fire burning more fire. But with Marian..."

Yes.

With Marian, it somehow worked, clicked, in a way I could never have predicted. The itch in me to take, to wield and to hold, it would never go away—and it would never be fully satisfied with a dominant who was just as hungry for dominion as me. But with Marian between us...Marian, the accidental obsession, the accidental beloved...

"Okay, but what if Marian doesn't want this? What if she doesn't want two separate dominants obsessed with her, possessive of her?"

Lox gave me a slow, wicked smile. A dimple dug into her right cheek.

"We'll never know if we don't ask her ourselves."

RAFE

From above, Sherwood Forest had been a knobby green mass barely worth looking at, and from the road, it had been nothing more than an environment to search, different from a shelled city or remote mountain village only in its appearance, not in its function. When I'd looked it at before today, I'd only seen the trees as obstacles to vehicles and sight lines, I'd only seen the streams and endless, searching tree roots as *terrain*, the messy, mossy chessboard I'd need to move my pieces on.

Today, I saw it differently.

Lox and I edged from the concrete shell of the house into a fern-choked tangle of growth, and I felt my shoes on the soft soil between the trees. We crept between thick cedars and firs until we reached a deer track by a stream, and I saw the labyrinth of nigh-invisible paths that spiderwebbed through the forest, only revealing themselves to someone who wasn't looking for the idea of what a path should look like, to someone who trusted that beyond a chink in the ferns might be a trail worth following.

This wasn't *terrain* at all. This was a world all in itself, an entire universe, and one that could only be perceived from its interior, from the forest floor as one pushed their way through.

No wonder the aerial surveys had turned up nothing.

Lox led me this way and that, over ropey tree roots and around fallen logs and under skeins of moss. We slipped the security net set by my colleagues as easily as rain slips through the trees to the ground, and we'd done it not with expensive tech or elaborate misdirection or anything other than Sherwood itself, dense and maze-like and impervious to the casual visitor.

We stopped near a steep slope overlooking a nest of fallen limbs and hemlock roots.

"Your phone," Lox said. It was the first thing she'd said to me since we'd left the house.

I handed it to her. I didn't hesitate, didn't stop to think about what this meant, because I already knew.

But as I put the phone in her waiting hand, my own hand lingered, my fingertips resting on her wrist, the glass of the screen cool against my palm. A soft rain began streaking down around us, and the world was filled with the pattering of raindrops on the leaves above, and on the ferns below.

This was it. The last step. And we both knew it. We both knew that I could snatch my phone and tear back to the house before the others made it there; we both knew that I could snatch it from her palm and then make a call that would end with Lox captured, or worse.

If I lifted my hand, then I was really doing this. I was leaving the mission, the CIA, my job.

My country.

One shift of my wrist, and I would become an enemy of the state. A mere few inches of space between my phone and my hand, and I'd no longer be a patriot, but a traitor.

I would be giving the entirety of my future and my life to Lox, and Marian too.

I lifted my hand, leaving the phone resting on Lox's palm. She cocked her arm and threw the phone as hard as she could into the tangle of dead wood and ferns below, and before it even landed, she turned and gave me a hard kiss on the mouth.

When she pulled back, her eyes were bright.

"It's going to be okay," she said, and I imagined she was saying it because she had no one to say it to her a year ago. I imagined she was saying it because she needed to hear it too.

"I know," I said. "I'm with you."

Another hard kiss. The long hair on the side of her face blew gently against my cheek as she bruised my lips with her own. After she pulled away, lips swollen and wet, she led me deeper into the forest.

And that's how easy it was to leave a life behind.

It was close to noon when we broke through the trees and saw the farmhouse. It appeared abandoned, but a keen eye could discern signs of recent use—a compression of the grass near the treeline, a shiny padlock dangling from the rusted latch of the barn door. And also the clump of irate hackers waiting for us just inside the barn.

"How did we miss this place?" I asked as we walked to the barn. I'd thought between me and the NSA and CISA agents on the job, we'd caught everything outside the trees that Lox's people could use, but apparently not.

"You would have found it eventually," Lox said. "But only through newly commissioned aerial, or maybe if you'd actually driven down this road yourself, because we had its online footprint scrubbed. Over here—it's time you meet everyone. Well, you already know Will."

We walked inside the barn, which was filled with cars, ATVs, and motorcycles, and it had to be said that no one looked particularly excited to see me, especially Will.

"Search him," a woman with long braids and a squadron tattoo on her upper arm said, and two men roughly my size shoved me against a Jeep and started patting me down.

I wasn't offended, but I was a little amused by it all. "Lox already did this," I volunteered. I'd allowed Lox to check me before we even left the house—I would have been professionally irritated if she hadn't—and so she already knew I had nothing on my person. I'd only had my phone, which was currently in a pile of deadfall as impenetrable as a cluster of those metal hedgehogs the Germans put on the beaches of Normandy.

"Lox is compromised when it comes to you," said the woman. She looked deeply unimpressed by everything about me.

"But my plan worked, didn't it, Jovanna?" Lox said.

"What plan?" I asked.

Lox looked at me. "Us," she said simply, and for a moment, the rest of the world disappeared.

It was only her and me and the atomic connection between us. Charged and indelible.

"For the record, I hated the plan," Jovanna said, jarring us back into the present moment, and I forced myself to think about more than just Lox and when I could have her to myself again. "He could have just as easily decided to turn you over to Lackland."

I had to agree. Much as I was grateful that Lox had come hoping to change my mind, it had been a foolish gamble on her part. It would have been smarter to disarm me, or even kill me. I could tell that I was already going to have my hands full going forward—keeping Robin Loxley safe seemed to be a full-time job.

The men, satisfied I wasn't be-ribboned with wires and taped trackers, stepped back, and I turned to face the group.

"Where's Marian?" I asked at the same time as Lox said, "I don't see Marian."

"I sent her ahead with Alana and Tinker," Will said. He gave me a look that let me know he'd gladly skewer my eyeballs with tiepins if given the chance. "We thought you'd prefer that, Lox. Just in case we have less time than we'd thought."

Lox nodded, and even I had to concede they'd done the right thing. It already endeared me to this odd group of traitors and thieves, that they were so protective of Marian.

"We need to scatter then," Lox said. "Like we planned. Does everyone know how they're getting there?"

"Where?" I asked. I was ignored.

"Yes," Will said, looking around at the group. Everyone was nodding, putting phones away, palming car keys. "We'll see you in a few days, Lox."

She saluted them and then jerked her head at me. "You're with me, spy boy. Let's go."

———

It was embarrassing how easily we left Sherwood, and then the peninsula itself. Lox and I argued—constantly—about the best way to keep ourselves hidden, about who would drive and who would navigate...and then periodically fucking in the back seat when the arguing turned us on, which was always.

But in the end, it wasn't even a contest between us and the NSA. Lox and I had once moved through war zones, burgeoning revolutions, failed states—escaping Sherwood was almost a game, and a child's one at that.

After a meandering route that took us east before we looped back west, we came to a small dock, left the car in the lot, and boarded a fishing boat crewed by men who looked like they'd spent too many years getting splashed by cold water. From there, it was a wave-tossed eighteen hours until we came ashore in a narrow inlet guarded by spruces, firs, and hemlock. The water was clear as the air, and the air was the cleanest thing I'd ever breathed in my life. The boat crew helped us onto the rocky shore with our bags, and then they pushed off the rocks and sailed back out to the open sea.

We were alone.

"Alaska?" I asked as Lox started walking. Just behind the treeline, there was a narrow dirt road, and on that road was parked a sturdy-looking truck.

"Yes," she said, and nothing else. And then we threw our things in the truck, found the keys tucked into the driver's side visor, and continued our journey.

The way to Lox's new hideout—and therefore the beginning of my new life—was long and winding. Wonderful. Recursive where for so long I'd been linear, oblique where I'd been direct. After I'd taken care of my life in D.C. via a burner phone supplied by Lox, there was nothing left for me to do but watch the trees move past the window and think about what would come next, about seeing Marian again. About what it might mean for the three of us to be together, and even the possibility of it was breathtaking. That somehow, Marian, Lox, and I made a closed circuit, a wreath of need and power, that we couldn't forge any other way. Not with any two of us together, not with any other versions of ourselves, but with the three of us as we were now.

I wanted what I'd felt that night at The Knot: the three of us twisted into one tangle, dominant, dominant, sub. And this time I wanted it forever.

After several hours of driving, we stopped at a small roadside hotel, and Lox checked us in as a Mr. and Mrs. Errol Flynn, which amused me greatly, and clearly gave the judgmental innkeeper the impression that we were having an affair. An impression I was sure we didn't help that night when I made Lox scream herself hoarse after I fucked her against the door to our room.

And then it was the next morning, and Lox told me we were getting close to the new compound. I used the time to scroll through some of the folders of Ys data she had—or at least the most damning—and tried to imagine what Lackland would do next. Lox also filled me in on how they'd been building this place over the last year, on how they'd chosen it because they could make the entire compound off-grid, and the cooler weather meant it would take far less energy to cool down the rigs—and mostly because it was remote as hell.

"You've needed help," I observed. Money and hacking only got a person so far—boats slipping through borders, construction on American soil (even if it was remote American soil), sourcing all the equipment for a backup computer farm—all of that required a person with connections.

"There's a woman called Nimue," Lox finally said. "She's been helping us."

"Merlin Rhys's wife?"

Lox looked surprised. "You know her?"

"Merlin Rhys used to be the single most important man in the world when it came to geopolitical events, Lox," I said. "I have an idea of what he's up to now."

Lox wasn't impressed with my sarcasm. "Okay, spy boy. So Nimue approached me soon after I left, and said she'd been friends with my parents before they'd died. She and Merlin offered to help with anything I needed, and while I had my father's castle in Sherwood, I knew we should have a backup location, both for the data and for us. And she's been like magic, honestly. Anything we've wanted, any problems we couldn't solve..." Lox lifted a shoulder. "She's some kind of wizard, I swear."

"That's what they used to say about Merlin," I said, settling back into the seat and watching the landscape pass by. Trees and mountains and meadows of sweet pink fire-weed. In all my travels, in my entire career, I'd never been here, and it was strange, but it almost felt like this had been my destination all along. Like every deployment, every mission, and every sleepless night had been leading me right to this place, right to this woman and her ferocious, uncompromising heart.

Right to Marian and the rest of our lives.

"What will I do?" I murmured, more to myself than to Lox, and she looked over at me.

"What do you want to do?"

I thought about this. I thought about the day I walked into the recruiter's office and stood in an hours-long line to fill out my DD Form 4, my father's watch on my wrist and my hands shaking as I picked the pen off the cheap laminate table. They hadn't been shaking with nervousness, but with *relief*, because there it had been, finally, the thing I'd craved since my father had died and my mother had brought me to a country that felt like a waiting place, an airlock to the rest of my life. My hands had shaken as I'd picked up the pen to write in my name because I was finally choosing, finally saying *this is my home, and this is so much my home that I'll give my life to it. Maybe even for it.*

I felt that same shakiness now as Lox slowed the truck and we turned onto a narrow road which unspooled through the trees like a dirt ribbon. My hands trembled, my breath shivered in and out.

Not fear, but relief, relief, relief. I hadn't left *home* behind, because instead of a country, home was Lox and Marian. Home was us and whatever mischief we got up to together.

"I don't know," I finally answered.

"There will be plenty for an ex-spy to do," Lox said. "If you want."

"You of all people should know that *spy* is hardly the right word for what I was."

She waved a hand off the truck's steering wheel. She didn't care. "I just want you to know that I'm not planning on keeping you locked up in a tower like Rapunzel. If we want to learn more about Ys—if we want to stop them one day—we'll need someone who knows how to do what you do."

"And Marian?" I asked. "Is she planning on playing Rapunzel?" It was hard to imagine Marian without Fitzwalter Green, without her *Forbes* spreads and tailored pantsuits and quests for familial atonement.

"Believe it or not, we haven't had much time to talk about it," Lox said dryly, "what with being on the run from the NSA and all." We'd managed to talk to her a few times, but cell coverage on the Pacific and in the wilds of Alaska was spotty at best, and the conversations had been far too short. "But before I went to the house so you'd release Will, I told her the same thing I just told you." Worry, such an unfamiliar thing to see on Lox's sharply delicate features, pulled her winged brows together and tightened her jaw. "I didn't want to kidnap you away from your lives, you know. I don't want to hold you hostage."

"I very much doubt you could make me do anything I didn't want to do," I told her frankly. "And Marian wouldn't have followed you if she wasn't ready to give up the rest of her life, which was only the company anyway."

"A company that meant the world to her," Lox said unhappily. "And try as I might, I can't see any way she won't have to give it up entirely while she's living with us."

I didn't either. Marian had appointed a proxy to run the company in her absence, claiming illness, but before long, more permanent changes would be needed. She could hardly run a multimillion-dollar corporation while the NSA was actively hunting for her, which after all of our disappearances from Sherwood, they certainly would be.

But.

"Marian isn't going to play tower princess any more than I am," I said, reaching over to slide my hand over Lox's thigh. She stiffened for a moment—neither of us were used to physical comfort, or any touch at all that wasn't related to war or sex—but then relaxed. "She'll find her new life, just as I will. We both chose this. We both chose *you*."

"I know," she said, her mouth twisting. "I just want to give you something that's worth that choice."

"You already have. Robin, you've given us yourself."

I only ever used her first name when I meant it—when we were fucking or fighting—and from this angle, I could see the way her chest rose as it caught on a breath, the way her long red lashes swept up and then back down again. I could see the slow way she swallowed, as if fighting back some powerful feeling.

"Thank you," she said.

"I love you," I said simply.

"I love you too. And I love her. And—I think—yes, this is it. Do you see it? Through the trees?"

It took another few yards, but then I saw it glinting through the branches and leaves, metal and glass and wood, all giant windows and steep angles to repel the inevitable snow.

But it was summer now, and so the house was sunk into a verdant meadow, green and fireweed-pink, surrounded by trees and linked by a path to a small lake. I thought I could see hints of other buildings around the lake, all built in the same style, and knew those must be houses and workspaces for the rest of the Merry Men, but all thoughts left my head as I caught a glimpse of movement through the floor-to-ceiling window at the front.

Bare feet, dark hair, a lilac sundress.

Marian.

FOURTEEN

RAFE

NEITHER LOX NOR I SPOKE, but I knew we were both feeling the same sudden rush of dark hunger, a hunger that we couldn't sate with each other no matter how hard we tried —although I'd be lying if I didn't say that the trying was still very enjoyable. But we still needed more and thirsted for more, and that more was Marian, it was her surrender, her willingness to crawl to the feet of us carnivores and show us her long, graceful throat.

The truck rolled to a stop, parked, turned off. And then there was only the clatter of seat belts and doors, and only us stalking up to the front door, both of us moving like predators who've just scented prey on the wind.

My cock was already thick and wedged against the zipper of my trousers, and my mouth watered for Marian, for Lox, for the three of us together. I wouldn't be able to wait once I got inside the house. I needed to fuck now. *Top now.*

"I hope she's ready," Lox said, voice full of dark promise, and then pushed open the front door and strode inside.

Marian was framed by the expanse of window behind her, turning when she heard us, her eyes as vivid as jewels. The dress she wore fell softly over her curves, and she wore no bra, so I could see the shape of her breasts and the pebbled juts of her nipples. The shadows of her thighs through the flimsy material.

She looked at us advancing on her, me in my Oxfords and Lox in her boots, and she gave us a wicked smile. "Green," she said, before we could say a single word.

This woman.

My stride was the longest and so I was the first to reach her. I seized her with one arm around her waist and curled my free hand around her jaw and kissed her, exploring the soft shape of her mouth with my own before pushing my tongue past her lips to remind myself of how she tasted.

"We missed you, darling," I murmured against her mouth. "Did you miss us?"

"Yes, sir," she panted. I kissed her again, hard, keeping her jaw in my grip as I did. She tasted clean and sweet, like summer itself, and her mouth was so giving, so soft and warm.

I couldn't wait to fuck it.

Lox was just behind me, and clearly impatient, because she tried to shove me out of the way, which was almost cute, given the extra foot and not negligible amount of weight I had on her. As a peace offering, I used my grip on Marian's jaw to turn her face to Lox's so Lox could kiss her too.

Because I still had Marian pressed tight to me, I could feel her respond to Lox's kiss, feel the way she swayed on her feet like kneeling was already on her mind, and my erection swelled even more against her, an ache gripping me deep in the balls.

"Jealous, Rafe?" Lox murmured, not lifting her mouth from Marian's to ask.

"Entirely so," I said, not letting go of Marian's jaw, but using the hand I had wrapped around her waist to hike up her dress. "Want to incite my jealousy even more?"

"I live to provoke you," said Lox.

"Then do something about this," I invited my fellow dominant, and Lox looked over Marian's shoulder to see the pert, knickers-less bottom there.

"Marian, you're not wearing anything under your dress," Lox said dangerously.

"I knew you were coming today," Marian breathed. Her pupils had dilated nearly to the edges of her irises; she looked drunk on kisses alone. "I've been lonely without you two."

"We've been lonely without you," I said, and Lox nodded, although her eyes seemed to be narrowing in thought, as if she were hatching one of her plans.

"We have to have you now," Lox said to Marian. Her hand had roamed down to Marian's backside, and her other hand was inside Marian's bodice, plundering the soft flesh she found there. "Red means stop. Say *yes* if you understand."

"Yes, Lox."

Lox pushed away from Marian and strode into the main living space, which stretched into a bright, open kitchen with a large island.

"Bend her over the island," Lox ordered, already hunting through the room, as if looking for something. I couldn't see anything but computer parts waiting to be assembled, monitors and cords and—

And cable ties.

Lox fisted a bundle of cable ties and walked toward the kitchen as I hauled Marian over my shoulder and carried her to the island. Her bare feet kicked up in the air before I dropped her down, spun her to face the island, and then bent her over it as Lox had asked.

"Please," Marian moaned as Lox shoved her skirt up around her waist. "*Please.*"

"*Please* what?" Lox said impassively. She ran a hand up Marian's thigh and then swatted her on the ass. "Seems to me that you're not in a position to be begging for anything."

"Kick her legs apart," I said. "See if she's wet."

Lox nudged Marian's bare feet apart, and I nearly groaned when I saw Marian's tight pink opening. She was more than wet—she was glistening and ready.

Lox pushed two fingers inside, and Marian arched, squirming, panting.

"Hold her," Lox said, and it was an order I was happy to obey. I walked to the side of the island and found Marian's wrists, pinning them to the marble as Lox probed inside her cunt. "So sweet inside here," she murmured to Marian. She pulled her fingers free and sucked them clean. "Tastes sweet too."

Marian whimpered, trying to squirm for more, but I had her secured against the marble too well. She was up on the balls of her feet, her hips flush to the edge of the counter, and with her arms stretched out in front of her and then pinned under my hand, the only thing she could move was her head.

"Needy," Lox observed. "Far too needy."

She took the cable ties in her hand and ran the stiff plastic tips up Marian's seam, making a disapproving noise at the way Marian bucked against them.

"We'll have to do something about it, I think," Lox said. "She needs reminding that sluts don't get to come until they've earned it."

"Spare the rod..." I said sagely, and with a fast and wicked grin, Lox brought up her hand and then whipped the cable ties across Marian's pert bottom. The cable ties weren't as long as the falls on a flogger, but they were long enough to have some give to them as they struck unsuspecting skin. Judging from the way Marian shivered, they must have felt much the same as a flogger, where the pain started slow and warm and itchy, and then slowly built and built as the strikes kept coming.

Lox snapped the ties against Marian's ass again, and the plastic made a bright, sharp sound as it bit into the skin. Again, she shivered, but she didn't jolt, or moan, or strain against where I held her wrists down. I lifted an eyebrow at Lox, who nodded back at me. She placed a hand over Marian's tailbone, eyed Marian like a painter eying a canvas, and then came down on exactly the same spot, harder than before.

Marian sucked in a breath, and before she could finish releasing it, Lox was switching her again, and again, and again. She paused only to move to Marian's other cheek, or to move down to Marian's thighs, and she kept her rhythm fast and even, not bothering to lull her submissive into relaxing, the way we usually would with impact play. It seemed she had the singular goal of cable-tying Marian's pretty bottom until it glowed pink and hot, and within a few minutes, she had her wish. My arms were long enough that I could hold Marian's wrists and still catch a glimpse of her backside, and the sight was enough to make my cock surge: swatches of deep pink, the color of the fireweed outside, textured with thin, narrow welts. And Lox wielded those cable ties like a master at work, her aim true and her force perfect, because now Marian was wholly lost to the feeling of Lox's punishment, her head rolling on the counter and her whimpers echoing against the marble. She pulled against my restraining hand and her feet kicked up over and over, until Lox trapped one leg with her own and merely dodged the other foot whenever it flew up to protect her now-beleaguered ass.

"Rafe," Marian panted. "Sir."

"Yes, sweet one?" I looked down at her, so beautiful like this, stretched over the counter and receiving her punishment, and it struck me that I rarely got to see this with a submissive. Usually, I would be in Lox's position, delivering the pain and pleasure, calibrating the strikes as I measured a submissive's reaction. I would be setting the scene, the pace, holding space for all of it and for ourselves, and while it was the singular craving of my soul to play like this, I couldn't deny that I sometimes wished I could have *more*, see more and feel more. To have the pleasure of seeing a sub's mouth fall open with bliss, of fully seeing their flinches and rolls and archings.

And now I could. I could see all of Marian's reactions and hear all her noises and get to feel the struggle against my grip as she pulled this way and that, trying to escape Lox's cable-tie-enabled sadism. And I loved it so much, I loved *Marian* so much, and I loved Lox, and that was another gift too, being able to see Lox at work with a submissive. See her when the power was able to flicker and flare from her in a bright, dancing burn, when we weren't so busy trying to swallow each other whole that we lost the chance to savor the taste.

Lox tossed the cable ties onto the counter, where they

scattered into a crosshatch of black plastic, and then cupped Marian's pussy with satisfaction plain on her face.

"Wet. Like a little whore," she said, and Marian moaned again, pushing her hips out for more of Lox's attention. Lox didn't give it to her; she held up her hand so I could see it glisten with how much Marian needed to come.

I let go of Marian's wrists and walked over to Lox. Taking Lox's wrist in my hand, I guided her wet fingers to my mouth and drew them in, tasting Marian on her skin. Heat crept up my thighs and settled deep in my groin at the taste, at the sheer hedonism of licking one lover off the skin of another.

I allowed Lox to pull her fingers free of my mouth, and then I turned my attention to the panting sub next to me. Her hair was tousled over her back, and I could see where her ribs moved in and out with quick breaths. Aroused breaths. Her cunt was wet and swollen, opened a little with need, and her bottom and thighs were gorgeously red and welted.

"It looks like you've enjoyed what Lox did to you," I said, petting a hand over Marian's abused skin. "I think you should thank her for it."

"Yes," whispered Marian. "Yes."

Lox needed no encouragement from me. She bent down and unlaced her boots, and then toed them off, making way for her trousers and tight black briefs to follow. And then— surprising me—she peeled off her tank top and sports bra underneath. Dominants didn't often prefer to be fully naked, at least not this early in a scene, and certainly not while a submissive was still clothed, but effortless power suffused her slender frame as she stepped over to the counter. Her bearing was unconsciously arrogant, her eyes bright with greed as I wrapped my hand around Marian's thick hair and urged her to straighten up.

Lox hopped on the counter and spread her legs in a silent command.

"Time to show your gratitude, darling," I told the submissive, and she bent forward eagerly, placing her hands on Lox's thighs for balance, and lowered her mouth to her work. I kept my hand in Marian's hair all the while and savored the tableau of kink on display in front of me. The welts, the fisted hair. The shameless service between Lox's thighs.

I savored the sight of Lox too, Lox as I'd so rarely seen her. The way we fucked was rough, urgent, the kind of sex that tumbled from nothing to everything in only a few seconds, and so we were both usually clothed or partially clothed. Nakedness was not something we'd had often between us, and I could probably count on one hand the times I'd seen that constellation of freckles near Lox's navel or the scar on her hip from a fall she'd taken in Ranger school. And getting to see so much of her all at once, when normally I only had glimpses as we'd changed clothes or showered while on assignment, was an indulgence, a profligacy when I so very much loved to be a profligate man.

"Like what you see?" Lox murmured when she caught me staring at her breasts and stomach. She leaned back on her hands, tilting her cunt up toward Marian's mouth and putting herself on display for me.

"I've never liked anything more," I said, looking at them both, server and served, heiress and thief.

Lox seemed to enjoy the frank voyeurism, because a dark flush moved up her chest and to her cheeks as she observed me observing her, and the tips of her breasts had bunched into tight little points, tight enough that they looked like they ached.

"She needs to come," I said to Marian. Just for fun, I nudged her bare feet apart with my shoe so I could look at her pussy while she had her face between Lox's legs. "And I know you don't want her to have to wait for something she needs."

Marian shook her head, a toss of dark hair that I felt in my fist since I was holding so much of it, and then began working even harder, her fingertips pressing into Lox's lean thighs as she gave Lox's cunt everything she had, sucks and licks and long, rimming kisses.

Lox swore, her head dropping back, one of her hands flying forward to join mine in Marian's hair, and then with a low exhale, she came, her fingers twisting next to mine, her belly quivering, her eyes closed in pure ecstasy. She was a work of art when she came, all the feral mischief and burning conviction sliding aside for a single instant to reveal the tender light of her soul, and something splintered inside me to watch it. Splintered and broke.

I couldn't wait anymore. I had to fuck.

Using the hand still wrapped in her hair, I lifted Marian's face from Lox's sex and marked those half-hooded eyes, those flushed cheeks. Like Lox, her nipples had turned taut and needy, and they poked from under her dress, tempting pinching fingers like my own.

Lox was still panting on the counter as I made quick work of Marian's dress, unzipping it, and then tugging it over the swell of her hips and down to the floor. "Tell me if we get to *red* or *yellow*," I told her, getting two cable ties from the abandoned pile on the counter.

"I will," she promised. Her eyes dropped to the cable

ties and she licked her lips. "Are you going to use those on me? Sir?"

"I'm going to bind your hands and your ankles and then I'm going to fuck you until my cock doesn't ache anymore."

"Oh," she breathed. "Okay."

"Green, then?"

"Green."

Lox watched me, lazy and sated, as I deftly cinched Marian's ankles together, and then her wrists. When I pulled back to admire my efforts, Lox and I both let out long, slow breaths.

Marian was fucking *beautiful* trussed up like this, bound and welted, her mouth wet and swollen from being fucked. I seized her and hauled her against me for a kiss.

I let out a ragged groan as I tasted Lox on her mouth. I tore away with a curse.

I wasn't going to last until I got to a bed at this rate.

I tossed Marian over my shoulder as Lox hopped gracefully off the counter. "Where's the bedroom?" I asked hoarsely, already moving out of the kitchen.

Marian squeaked as we started walking, unable to catch her balance with her wrists bound, dangling over my shoulder like a helpless captive. "Up the stairs," she managed, and I walked toward the floating staircase with long, impatient strides, taking the steps two at a time when I reached them.

Upstairs, the house was no less light-filled and modern than it was below. Large windows looked out onto the lake and the woods, and a hooded balcony beckoned from the end of the sleekly furnished bedroom. I ignored it. My attention belonged only to the warm CEO slung over my shoulder and to the thief padding silently behind us. To the low bed, neatly made with white sheets and blankets. They begged to be rumpled and twisted.

I set Marian down on the bed, balanced her on her knees and elbows, and then unzipped my trousers, my eyes on the heart shape of her backside and the narrow valley between her thighs, wet and lined with pink. Her bound ankles meant that her thighs were pressed tightly together, and my erection pushed eagerly against my boxer briefs as I anticipated how snug her pussy would be for me like this.

"Let me," Lox said, pushing my hand away and tugging down the waistband of my boxer briefs herself. I hissed when she took my aching length in her grip, hissed again when she found the pre-cum at my head and used it to give me two rough, slick strokes. I was only a step or two away from the edge of the bed, but she pulled me there by my cock anyway, probably to annoy me. Which succeeded.

My irritation resulted in one of her wicked grins.

"The big, bad wolf doesn't like being led around by his big, bad dick?" Lox asked innocently, and Marian laughed on the bed.

I grabbed Lox by the waist and yanked her close. For all her strength and fire, she was easy enough for me to manhandle, and I let her feel my strength as she braced both of her hands against my chest and fought against my grip. I let her feel my power as I brought my mouth slashing over hers.

She kissed me fiercely as she struggled to get free, as if trying to win on both fronts, and then, bit by bit, she was seduced deeper into the kiss, letting my tongue inside her mouth, digging her fingernails into my chest instead of trying to push me away. Once I felt her soften against me, her naked curves pressed to my clothed body, I let her go. I did it so abruptly that she stumbled back a step. She glared at me.

Marian, watching over her shoulder, laughed.

"The clever little fox doesn't like being led around by her filthy little mouth?" I asked, also innocently.

"Very funny," Lox said. "But you're forgetting that I know the one thing that drives you more than dominance."

She'd stepped close to me again, and I was momentarily distracted by the high, firm curves of her breasts. "And what's that?" I murmured with my eyes trailing all over her body.

She gave me a smug look. "*Greed*."

And then she took hold of my erection and guided me right to Marian's waiting hole.

The moment the crown pressed against the warm opening, I lost all sense of myself. Lox was right, she'd always be right, because I was greedy above all else, greedy to have and greedy to take. Greedy to feel every inch of a lover all at once, and greedy to pillage every last bit of what they would offer up to me.

Marian let out a low moan as—still guided by Lox—I began to shove my way inside. Marian was wet enough to take me, but with her ankles cinched together, it was work getting myself inside her pussy. Crude thrusts that still only gained me a little bit each time, even when I curled my hands around Marian's hips to pin her in place.

Lox let go of me to reach around Marian's hip and push her fingers between Marian's thighs. I knew that there wasn't room to play with her clit, not really, but Marian was so frantic to come that whatever Lox did manage to do had her whimpering and whining for more.

"What do you think, Rafe?" Lox asked me, in the same tone of voice she might ask me about the weather, despite her nakedness and despite the fact that I was currently trying to wedge my way inside her girlfriend. "Should we let her come?"

"Not yet," I grunted. "Want her wild for it."

"I'm already wild for it, I promise," panted Marian. "Please, sir. Please, please—"

"Shh," Lox said. "You'll only make it worse for yourself."

After all that toil, I finally slid all the way into our submissive, pressing until my hips were flush with her ass and I was fully hilted. Her channel was all silken heat, all slickness and squeeze, and when I punched my hips forward, I could feel the resulting ripple and clench of her inner muscles around me, like her body was trying to clutch me closer to her.

Lox swept her hand through Marian's hair and gave her a swift kiss on the temple, and then crawled up to the top of the bed, where she arranged herself against the padded headboard and parted her legs.

Even though I'd just seen the secret parts of her body downstairs—even though we'd spent the last two days fucking every chance we could—seeing her expose herself so deliberately, so brashly, sent fire roiling through me. She ran a finger up the line of her sex, tracing a path from the tight, pink eyelet of her ass over the petals of her inner labia, and then stopping at her clit.

"Are you teasing me?" I asked hoarsely. I couldn't move inside Marian, because I knew I'd come if I did, feeling Marian and watching Lox fuck herself at the same time.

"Maybe I'm the one being teased," Lox said archly, giving me and Marian a pointed look.

This didn't bother me in the least, because I liked knowing I was getting to her. Besides, I was having too much fun where I was.

"Still green?" I murmured to Marian, and she nodded, her dark hair draped down around her face like a veil as she did. I reached forward—a movement that had us both inhaling as it made my cock flex inside her—and carefully swept the hair away from her face, tucking it behind her ear and then around her neck. I wanted to see her face when I fucked her.

"Still green, sir," she replied. "Fuck me, please."

In response, I gave her already welted ass a hard spank, pulled out, and then rammed home, rough enough to make her cry out. And that cry tore apart the last shred of control I had—deep, animal need clawed at the base of my spine, telling me to *fuck*, to *come*, and I obeyed. I pulled out again and began pumping in and out with mindless urgency, feeling the heat of her abused bottom against my hips, seeing the fast, hectic jerks of her ribs as she panted, watching the flush bloom so deep and rosy on her cheeks that I wondered if I'd be able to taste it.

She was beautiful and full of surrender and her cunt was so hot and tight and right—and Lox was there in front of us, regal as royalty, feral as ever, chin up, eyes hooded, fingers working lazily between her thighs.

The climax thundered through me, and every muscle in my body, from my toes to my jaw, clenched as the orgasm unleashed itself in torrents and booms, a never-ending surge and retreat as I swelled impossibly harder and then began unloading inside her.

She was fucking back against me as much as she could, and I was rutting into her like a beast, over and over again, my cock seizing and jerking, flooding her with my release and making everything even slicker, even wetter.

"Shit," Lox said, her gaze fixed on where I was penetrating our submissive. Her fingers worked her clit even faster, her other hand rolling a breast—hard, the way I'd do it if I could reach her.

I didn't stop pounding Marian's pussy until I was all the way drained, and even then I didn't stop, needing more, needing *again*, needing her until she was wrecked beyond reckoning and my obsession with her was fed...for the moment, at least.

I pulled out suddenly, enjoying the pearly drips of my orgasm leaking from her as I did, and then I found the pocket knife I kept in my pocket. With a flick of my thumb and a quick, careful cut, Marian's ankles were no longer fettered by the cable tie. I closed the knife, put it back in my pocket, and then finally undressed.

Like a good submissive, Marian stayed put without being told, her cunt still visibly used, her cheeks flushed, and her eyes frenzied as she watched me. "You look like you're about to beg me for something," I told her, palming her ass and then a tit before mounting the bed and settling next to Lox, who was still watching us like we were putting on a show just for her pleasure.

Marian lifted her head to look at us both, and still braced on her elbows and knees like this, she looked like a supplicant at court, crawling to a king and queen for mercy.

"Please, sir," she pleaded. Her eyes slid to Lox, and she whispered, "Lox. Please let me come."

Lox rolled her head on the headboard to look at me. "What do you think?"

"I think she's very, very pretty like this," I replied, not taking my eyes off the trembling, well-fucked submissive in front of me. "It makes it quite hard to want her any other way."

Lox's voice was dark when she said, "I agree."

Marian whimpered.

"But I suppose she has behaved for us, hasn't she?"

"She has."

"What about this, darling?" I said to Marian. "If you can come just from riding me, then you can have your orgasm, and another one as a reward."

"And if I can't?" Marian asked breathlessly.

I looked to Lox.

"Then you'll have to wait until tonight," Lox decided. "*Late* tonight. Maybe even technically tomorrow morning."

"She's cruel," I said to Marian in a conspiratorial tone. "But what can I do? I love her so. Now come here and show us how badly you want it."

Neither Lox nor I moved to help Marian as she raised herself to her knees and then shuffled up to us. With her wrists still cable-tied together, her movements were halting and clumsy, and Lox and I watched her with the same dark satisfaction that spiders must watch little bugs struggle in their webs. Finally, she made it to us and lifted her knee to straddle my hips. My cock—harder than steel, burning like a newly cast sword—leapt up to graze against her soft pussy. But I didn't move to slot it against her hole. I didn't help her at all, in fact, and when she looked up at me with that helpless expression, I only smiled and tucked a hand behind my head. The other arm went around Lox, to pull her close.

"I think you're on your own," Lox observed, and Marian huffed.

Lox smacked her ass for it, and Marian yelped, falling forward onto my chest with her bound hands.

"Ready to behave?" I asked sternly, and Marian nodded against my chest, her hair sliding and tickling so sweetly over my bare skin.

It took her a moment to find the right angle, the right

way to swivel her hips, but she was slick enough and I was hard enough that once she got there, she could impale herself easily.

Once she had me seated inside, she straightened up—hair mussed, rose-colored nipples jutting through the dark tresses—and began riding me with sharp, hungry movements of her hips, riding my cock like her life depended on it. Her cunt was so good, *too* good, and despite all my dispassionate playacting, I was already skating on the edge of pumping her full a second time. Especially after Lox leaned forward and threaded her hand through Marian's hair, pulling her in for a long, silken kiss while Marian fucked herself on my cock with eager bucks and long, grinding circles.

"Watch, little fox," Lox said, settling back and parting her legs again, so Marian could see as Lox slid her fingers deep into her sex and used the wetness there to start masturbating herself. "I love watching you get topped," Lox said. "It gets me so hot. Even if I'm not the one doing it. Ah, that's so good, baby, keep doing it just like that. Make yourself come. You want to come, don't you? You want to feel better?"

"Yes," said Marian in a sex-hazed mumble. "Yes, Lox."

"Then show us. Show me. Show me what a good girl you are."

I could feel Marian tightening around me, and I could feel her thighs quivering, *see* the quiver in her belly, and she angled herself the tiniest bit forward to make sure her clit got the friction it needed—and I was fighting with every ounce of strength I had not to come yet, to keep myself utterly still—

With a cry, she broke apart around my erection, shivering on top of me and slumping forward onto my chest as contractions rocked her body and sent flutters along my throbbing shaft.

I cursed, unable to hold back, and banded my arms around her back as I jackknifed up with my hips, driving into her over and over again until my balls pulled tight to my groin and then I began pumping her full. Again.

Next to us, Lox came too, back arching off the headboard as her body curved with the force of her orgasm, and somehow it still wasn't enough, not enough to sate the raw hunger inside. I flipped Marian onto her back, her bound arms coming to rest behind her head, and then I dove between her legs, needing to lick her clean, needing to feel her come on my tongue.

"Ah, there's the reward he promised," Lox said huskily. "You were such a good girl, weren't you? You've earned this."

"Yes," Marian said, sounding dizzy. "Oh God, it feels so good, Lox. Oh—oh—"

Lox kissed her while I ate her out, and there was something so perfect about it, being wet and tangled together, messy kisses above and below, and when Marian came against my mouth, I was already getting hard again, ready for more, even though I knew it would ache later.

Lox laughed as I emerged from Marian's legs with a renewed erection. "Oh Marian, you've created a monster. You better return the favor."

Marian was utterly spent, her arms still above her head, her breasts and soft stomach moving as she panted. "Why can't you?" she asked Lox, and I snorted as Lox gave a sharp smile and then clicked her teeth.

"I bite," she said simply.

It was true.

"You don't need to move, darling," I told Marian,

approaching her on my knees and then taking my arousal in hand and pressing the head to her mouth. "Just let me use you for a minute."

And it was really only a minute. With her plush, full lips, her curious tongue, her hot mouth—not to mention the extremely pleasant sight of both her and Lox utterly naked and utterly wrecked, I was coming nearly immediately, shoving all the way in and pouring down her throat.

When at last I'd had my fill of her and the scene, I pulled free and kissed her on the mouth. She tasted like all of us now, and I wanted to keep it that way forever.

"Hold still," I ordered and moved off the bed to get the knife again. I cut the cable tie binding her wrists, put the knife away, and then began rubbing the irritated marks from where the plastic had dug into her skin.

Lox got off the bed and went to the en-suite, returning with a cool, damp washcloth. Together we rolled Marian onto her stomach, and I continued to massage her wrists while Lox gently soothed Marian's reddened backside with the cloth.

"How are you doing, little fox?" Lox asked her.

"Perfect," Marian said dreamily. "Completely perfect."

Lox stroked her back. "You deserve to feel perfect, because you are." She looked at me. "Shower time?"

"I should think so."

***

IT WAS strange having another dominant giving aftercare alongside me, but it was the kind of strange that felt like an answer to a question I'd long ago forgotten how to ask. It felt like an answer to the past year, to my entire life, to the rest of my life. Lox and I helping wash Marian, wrapping her in blankets, pulling her into our arms as we arranged ourselves in bed with her between us. I was stroking her damp hair, and she was holding Lox's hand, when I finally found the courage to ask.

"Do you want to do this?" I asked Marian in a low voice. "I know that between us—well, it's been fast," I continued.

But Marian didn't hesitate. "Yes, I want to do this, Rafe. Do you?"

"It's the only thing I want to do."

Lox exhaled slowly with relief. Maybe she'd been worried about this, deep down. That while the bonds between her and me, and her and Marian, were forged in something unbreakable and everlasting, the thing between Marian and me was still too tender and new to build a future on.

"I love you," I went on. "And the reason I know this can last is because this is how I fell in love with Lox. Right away and completely."

Marian looked up at me and then pressed her lips to my throat. "I love you too, sir."

"Lox and I both loving you will be a lot."

"I wouldn't have it any other way," she said, and Lox laughed.

"Good."

After some more making out, and after Lox gave Marian a final orgasm, we were all tucked in for the evening, Marian draped across my chest asleep, and Lox's eyes glittering in the Alaskan summer midnight.

"There's one thing I still can't figure out," Lox said, quietly so as not to wake Marian. "How did you even find Marian in the first place? How did you know she'd be at The Knot?"

"Mark Trevena," I said, and she gave a small flinch.

"I bet that information didn't come for free," she said.

"It never does."

"What did you give him in return?"

I adjusted myself so that I was lying flat and I pulled Marian closer. Across the elegant contours of her back, I found Lox's hand and slid my own into it.

"Something about a girl named Isolde." And then I yawned, worn out by the last few weeks and ready to start my new life with these two perfect people, my two obsessions, my two hearts. Lox yawned too and snuggled against me and Marian.

"Sounds intriguing," she murmured, and I thought briefly of what I'd told Mark about the young woman. I hoped he'd taken the warning I'd given him along with that information to heart.

"I think in this case, that's not a good thing."

"Unlike us, you mean," said Lox, and I could hear the smile in her voice.

I smiled too. *Intriguing* was the least of the words I would use to describe the tangled, thieving love that had sprung up between her, Marian, and me.

"Unlike us, Robin."

And she sighed that sigh she made whenever I used her first name, and whatever came next—whatever Lackland tried and whatever we learned about Ys—I knew we'd at least have this. Sighs in the night and slow touches in the dark.

Forever with the three of us—greedy, twisted, wicked.

And it would be perfect.

The End.

Love a fairy tale with a kinky, ménage twist?

Check out ***American Queen***, the first in my kinky, queer King Arthur retelling where Guinevere, King Arthur, and Lancelot find a *very dirty* happily ever after—together!

And I promise I'm not done with Mark Trevena—or Isolde. Or Ys!

The first time I meet the devil, he knows my name.

The second time I meet him, the truth becomes clear: Mark Trevena is to be my husband.

No matter that we don't know each other. No matter that

he's older than me; shameless and sinful; the owner of a secret club where the powerful come to play. My father has spoken, and I'll be the devil's bride the minute I graduate from college.

Except my future husband has one condition for this arranged marriage: we have to pretend it's real.

He'll teach me, he says. How to pretend to be his in pain and pleasure both.

How to pretend to arch and writhe under his touch. But his lessons are teaching me something else entirely...

...that Mark Trevena wants me in a way that's not pretend at all.

And no matter how I might fight it, the devil will have his due.

Check out the first book in the Lyonesse series for completely free!

both times ended in gutting heartbreak. Now she's sworn off all romance forever, determined to teach her classes and do her research, and live out the rest of her days alone.

I want to be his everything.

But Ash Colchester hasn't sworn off Greer--not at all. Still in love with the girl he once kissed in a circle of broken glass, this soldier-turned-President has never forgotten the taste of her kisses or the sound of her whispered, *yes, please* against his mouth. He's never forgotten the promises he wanted to make her and couldn't because she was too young for him then, and far too innocent for the things he needs. But he can't wait any longer . . .

But can a fairy tale have a happily ever after for three people?

Desperate to have her, Ash sends his best friend Embry to bring Greer to him, not knowing they have their own secrets, their own tragedies together. Their own cravings . . .

Soon, Greer finds herself caught between past and present, pleasure and pain--and the two men who long for each other as much as they long for her. And as war and betrayal press ever closer, they tumble headlong into a passionate love affair that will change the world.

My name is Greer Galloway and I serve at the pleasure of the President of the United States.

And now I've returned, hopeful...and wary. Because it's so very easy to be drawn back into the world of the seductive and elegant Auden Guest . . . and into the world of his worst enemy, St. Sebastian Martinez. The beautiful and brooding St. Sebastian is as irresistible as he ever was, and Auden is just as handsome and arrogant, and the three of us can't seem to unknot ourselves from each other.

From the hasty promise we three made all those years ago.

As Thornchapel slowly tightens its coil of truths and lies around us, our reluctant threesome starts unravelling into filthy, holy pleasure and pain. Together we've awakened a fate that will either bloom like a rose . . . or destroy us all.

Learn More About A Lesson in Thorns and the Wild,
Wicked Secrets of Thornchapel!

ALSO BY SIERRA SIMONE

Co-Written with Julie Murphy:

A Merry Little Meet Cute

Snow Place Like LA: A Christmas in July Novella

A Holly Jolly Ever After

Seas and Greetings

A Jingle Bell Mingle

Fundamentals of Being a Good Girl

The Lyonesse Trilogy:

Salt in the Wound (a free Lyonesse prequel!)

Salt Kiss

Honey Cut

Bitter Burn

Standalones:

Red & White: an FFM winter story — FREE!

Supplicant: an age gap novella

Sanguine: an MM vampire story

Sherwood: an FFM novella

My Present This Year: a forbidden Christmas story - FREE!

The Priest Series:

Priest

Midnight Mass: A Priest Novella

Sinner

Saint

Prodigal Son

Thornchapel:

A Lesson in Thorns

Feast of Sparks

Harvest of Sighs

Door of Bruises

Misadventures:

Misadventures with a Professor

Misadventures of a Curvy Girl

Misadventures in Blue

The New Camelot Trilogy:

American Queen

American Prince

American King

The Moon (Merlin's Novella)

American Squire (A Thornchapel and New Camelot Crossover)

High Spice Historicals:

The Markham Hall Series

The Awakening of Ivy Leavold

The Education of Ivy Leavold

The Punishment of Ivy Leavold

The London Lovers

The Seduction of Molly O'Flaherty

The Wedding of Molly O'Flaherty

Far Hope Stories

The Chasing of Eleanor Vane

The Last Crimes of Peregrine Hind

The Conquering of Tate the Pious

Co-Written with Laurelin Paige

Porn Star

Hot Cop

About the Author

Sierra Simone is a USA Today bestselling former librarian who spent too much time reading romance novels at the information desk. She lives with her husband and family in Kansas City.

Sign up for her newsletter to be notified of releases, books going on sale, events, and other news!

www.thesierrasimone.com
thesierrasimone@gmail.com

www.ingramcontent.com/pod-product-compliance
Lightning Source LLC
Chambersburg PA
CBHW011139190726
48289CB00012B/3080